MW01172636

Holiday Ever After

USA TODAY BESTSELLING AUTHOR

J.D. HOLLYFIELD

Holiday Ever After
Copyright © 2021 J.D. Hollyfield

Cover Design: All By Design
Photo: Deposit Photos
Editor: Word Nerd Editing
Proofing: Novel Mechanic

ALL RIGHTS RESERVED. This book contains material protected under International and Federal Copyright Laws and Treaties. Any unauthorized reprint or use of this material is prohibited. No part of this book may be reproduced or transmitted in any form or by any means, electronic or mechanical, including photocopying, recording, or by an information and retrieval system without express written permission from the Author/Publisher.

This is a work of fiction. Names, characters, places, and incidents either are the product of the author's imagination or are used fictitiously, and any resemblance to actual persons, living or dead, business establishments, events, or locales is entirely coincidental

'Tis the season for falling in love with this hilarious, heart-warming, second-chance holiday romance.

Down on her luck, all Holly wants for Christmas is for her life to stop unraveling.
The last thing on her to-do list is traveling back to her hometown of Willow Falls. In fact, it's a place she's avoided for the past five years.

After being dumped by her boyfriend and fired from her job, stringing twinkle lights, decorating the tree, and sipping hot cocoa with her family turns out to be just what she needs to get out of her funk.

Until a familiar face from her past reappears, wreaking havoc on her life once again.

Liam Cody.

The one who got away.

The boy who shattered her heart and ran off with the pieces years ago.

But one glance at Liam, and all she sees is a strong, confident, sex God of a man. And the worst part? Her heart doesn't understand he doesn't belong to her anymore.

As the days tick down to Christmas, can Holly let go of the past and still get her kiss under the mistletoe?

more from
J.D. Hollyfield

Dirty Little Secret Duet
Bad Daddy
Sweet Little Lies

Love Not Included Series
Life in a Rut, Love not Included
Life Next Door
My So Called Life
Life as We Know It

Standalones
Celebrity Dirt
Faking It
Love Broken
Sundays are for Hangovers
Conheartists
Junkie
Chicks, Man
Lake Redstone

Paranormal/Fantasy
Sinful Instincts
Unlocking Adeline

#HotCom Series
Passing Peter Parker
Creed's Expectations

Exquisite Taste

2 Lovers Series
Text 2 Lovers
Hate 2 Lovers
Thieves 2 Lovers

Four Father Series
Blackstone

Four Sons Series
Hayden

At Christmas, all roads lead home.
-Marjorie Holmes

Chapter one

"Yes, Mom... I know, Mom... Trust me, if I could, I would. I'm *so* swamped at work." I glance at my vanity, searching for anything sharp to stab my eyes out.

It's always the same conversation. The same questions. *How's work? How's that boyfriend of yours? When is he going to propose? When are you coming home?* I don't even think she breathes between questions.

"I just don't understand who doesn't give their employees off for Christmas, honey. You've worked the holiday four years in a row."

"I know, Mom. Things are just really busy. I can't take off now."

She sighs.

It's no ordinary sigh. It's a mother's sigh with hidden meaning. The infamous Margaret Bergner sigh. The *if your brother were still alive, he would come home to be with his family for the holidays* sigh. Which is not to be confused with her *I expected more of you* sigh. Or the *shame, I was really depending on you* sigh. My mother has a whole book of sighs. But this one is the worst.

"Mom, I'm sorry. I want to be with you and Dad, but now isn't a good time."

And it's *not*. Guilt tickles at my conscience. But not

enough to change my mind. "Maybe when things settle down after the holidays."

"Speaking of settling down. . ." Dammit. I walked right into that one. "Your father was really hoping to meet Vincent."

Vincent. I haven't heard that name in a while. Maybe because he goes by so many other names now. Cheater. Bastard. Douchetard. That's Eileen's nickname.

"You know, you two have been together for three years. I'm not understanding why he hasn't proposed yet. You're not getting any younger, Holly." Ah, there it is. The monthly reminder. That's always my favorite. Almost twenty-six and not married. Way to rub it in.

"I know, Mom. Listen, I really need to get to work. I have a *huge* meeting today and really need to concentrate. Tell Dad I love him. I'll call you guys later in the week. Love you—"

"Oh, honey, before you hang up, I wanted to tell you I saw Liam the other day." Just when I think I've made it out alive, she throws a grenade at me.

My phone slips out of my hand, and I perform an impressive juggling act until I finally bring it back to my ear. "What do you mean you saw him? When did he get back?" He's back? He's back... *He's back...* "Thought he was stationed in some country doing Peace Corps stuff?"

"A few months ago—"

"*A few months!*—I mean, wow…three months." Thanks for the heads up, *Mom*.

"Looks very healthy. He's helping your father run the hardware store."

Liam Cody.

My high school sweetheart.

The love of my life.

More importantly, the one who hates my guts.

"Well, that's great, Mom. Okay, I *really* need to—"

"He asked about you."

Dammit! My phone slips out of my hand again. I really should have reconsidered returning those air pods Vincent bought me. "Wait...hello? Hi. He asked about me? Like, what do you mean *asked* about me?" Asked, as in he's hoping I'm rotting in hell somewhere?

"Well, he asked how you were, of course. I just couldn't stop bragging about how well you're doing. He told me to say hello the next time I talked to you."

I pause for a second until my brain catches up, then burst out into a fit of laughter. "He told *me* hello?" *Remember to Google negative meanings for hello.*

"Of course. Such a nice man. It's a shame you two never worked out."

"Yeah, shame," I say. Screw it. Google it now. *Negative meaning of—*

"Remind me again what went wrong between the two of you."

Would she like the long story or the cliff notes when he called me a selfish, conceited brat just before I told him to go to hell?

"Don't remember, Mom. Such a long time ago. Really gotta go. Love you. Give Dad my best. Bye." I hang up. Thank God the couch is behind me because otherwise, I would fall straight back against the floor.

"Are you ever going to tell your parents you lost your job?"

I turn to Eileen, my roommate. "Why would I do a crazy thing like that?" I reach for the remote and my box of donuts.

Eileen shrugs. "I mean... it's been a month. Maybe it's time. Maybe going home would be a good thing. As would be possibly showering."

3

I gasp at her. How dare she judge my choices. "What exactly are you trying to say?"

"That you're starting to smell and need to shower. You've been in those pajamas for four days now, and if I see you watch *The Notebook* one more time, I'm going to blow my brains out."

"Hey! *The Notebook* is one of the best love stories ever."

"Yeah, and watching you cry the entire time is ruining it for me."

I scoff at her. "I don't cry every time."

"Yes, you do."

"No, I don't!"

"Fine. Whatever. But you need to stop sulking. You lost your job, and Vincent cheated on you. I get it. It sucks. But he was a total douche, and that job worked you too hard. Maybe this is a good thing. A way to start fresh. Find somebody who appreciates you."

I sag further into the couch. The lump in my throat resurfaces, and tears prick my eyes. Three years I dedicated my life to Vincent, only for him to cheat on me with his trashy secretary. His reasoning was the best part of it all. She understood his sexual needs and fetishes. *Fetishes!* What did he want from her that I couldn't do? I would suck on toes. *Gross, no, I wouldn't.* Whips and chains? *Meh, I don't do pain well.*

"You really want to sulk over a guy who probably dreams about shoving a hamster up his—"

"Stop this absolute instant." I almost crawl out of my skin at the thought. I squeeze my eyes shut, cringing. "Gross. You're seriously not helping, you know."

"Well, you moping around watching cheesy romance flicks and eating your weight in powdered donuts won't make anything better. Vincent's a jerk. He lost the best thing that's ever happened to him."

I grab a throw pillow and clutch it to my chest. He is a jerk. And he didn't deserve me. To be really honest, Vincent wasn't great. He was a typical guy who showed affection when I needed it and kept me company instead of being alone. He was my distraction.

Maybe going home will do me some good. I can't remember the last time I indulged in the warmth and joy of Christmas—a holiday Vincent hated. A holiday that brought up too many memories. A holiday I avoided at all costs. But maybe it's time.

"Fine."

"Fine, as in you'll shower? Or fine as in you'll go home for Christmas?"

"Both." I press my nose to my armpit. "Definitely shower first."

Chapter two

A tightness forms in my chest as we pass the welcome sign for Willow Falls. Inhaling a deep breath, I take in the familiar scenery. It's been five years, and still nothing has changed when it comes to holiday traditions. And this town lives for the joy of Christmas. Over-the-top houses sparkle with an array of lights and figurines. There's not a roof without a Santa at the chimney, and if you're missing a reindeer, they sure as hell talk about you at church. Rudolph's nose is glowing a bright shade of red, just as it has since I could remember. Dad used to always say it's how Santa found our house. God forbid the year the light went out and I tried climbing out of my window to the roof while holding a flashlight so Santa wouldn't miss us.

We pull up to my childhood home. A thick layer of fluffy snow covers the ground, but not enough to hide Jesus and his manger display. An array of elves litter the bushes, carrying piles of glittery wrapped presents. Every decoration brings back memories. Being grounded for trying to unwrap the gifts. Scaring my parents to death when I was five, and they thought someone had kidnapped me, but I was sleeping in the miniature stable because I wanted to be just like Jesus. The ridiculous lights. So many—

"Unless you want me to escort you to the door, this is your stop, little lady."

I blink and pull my eyes away from the glowing house to the driver. "Sorry. Thanks for the offer, but I got it." I hold my breath and push open the door. I can't believe Eileen talked me into this.

It will be good for you.

Holidays should be spent with family.

You've hit rock bottom and need a reset.

I completely disagree with the last part. I have *not* hit rock bottom. It's called mourning. Look it up. The death of my perfect life. I had the perfect job as senior creative designer at one of the top advertising agencies in the city. It took me years to get there, and I was the best. Not only was my job amazing, but I also got to work side by side with my boyfriend, the director of brand management, Vincent Sheshull. We were unstoppable. Had the same aspirations. Goals. Work was our passion. We were both driven—me toward furthering my career, him toward boning his secretary.

It probably didn't help that I lost my cool at work and threw a few sluggers at her. And, okay, maybe HR getting involved wasn't the best. Turns out, no matter how good you are at what you do, assaulting another employee is frowned upon.

So, there was that. I walked out with a box of my things, my plant, and my pride. Well, the last one was in shambles. Still, I kept my chin up and had no regrets when I gave the entire building a fuck off speech, claiming my *now* ex had a small dick and couldn't get it up in case anyone else wanted to take a ride. I might have had tiny regrets. That outburst may have cost me a referral. But I'd just lost the best job of my life, money, a steady income—and my heart was in a million devastated pieces.

We had plans.

I mean, *I* had a plan. We weren't perfect. There were

doubts here and there… maybe more than there should have been, but we were going to get married. I felt it. I felt… something. *Yeah, anger, betrayal, murder…*

When you get thirty days with nothing but time on your hands, your mind conjures up the most creative ideas. We truly don't give our brains enough credit. It's a good thing I don't have it in me to disassemble a body or the muscle mass to drag one into the woods. Instead, I sulked. And sulked. And now, worse than being dumped like yesterday's trash, I'm parked outside my childhood home, about to spend the holidays with my parents, who still think my life is perfect.

"Those sure are some decorations. That's the holiday spirit if I say so."

Or desperation to contact aliens on Mars. "Yeah, my parents just love Christmas."

Climbing out, I grab my two suitcases from the trunk and tug them up the driveway, slipping on the ice and almost eating the frozen blacktop. I must resemble a shotty ice skater as I slip and slide up the walkway. I just about take out an elf and curse when the heel of my stiletto snaps.

"Bad idea. *Bad* idea." I should have stayed home. Ordered in Christmas dinner. Made sure my couch wasn't lonely. *Your family needs you. You need them too.* Shut up, conscience! I remember my mom's voice when I told her I was coming home, which makes the guilt surface again, knowing how selfish I've been the past five years. With my brother gone, I'm their constant concern.

This is right. I need to be here for them. The look on my mom's face when she sees me… she's probably going to cry and stuff me with Christmas cookies before I can even get my jacket off. I'm shocked she wasn't stalking the window for my arrival.

I drag my suitcases up the porch steps to the front door. Get through the holidays, then I can be home putting my life back together. I hope Mom made my favorite—the gingerbread cookies with the sprinkle buttons.

I turn the knob and push open the door. "I'm home!" I sing, waiting for my first cookie. The overwhelming scent of sugar. The crackling of the fire. *A Christmas Story* playing in the background.

There's nothing.

No cookies.

No smells.

Nothing.

"Hello? Mom? Dad?"

I'm met with silence. "What the...? Hello? Anyone home? I'm here!" I kick off my heels and look around. There has to be a mistake. Did I give them the wrong time? I grab my phone and pull up the email I sent Mom. Nope, it's right. Where the heck are they? I drop my suitcases and shimmy out of my jacket, tossing it on the back of the couch as I walk through the house. I gaze at the missing fire and head into the kitchen. Not a single sheet of cookies, just a note.

Holly,
Dad and I are at the hardware store.
Mom.

Am I seeing things? My parents, who have been dying for me to come home, aren't here to greet me? Dropping the note, I head to my old room, throw myself on my bed, and stare up at the glow-in-the-dark stars. I loved these stars as a kid. My brother Billy spent an entire day jumping up and sticking them perfectly so they would resemble a map of the galaxy. Every night, we would lay in my bed, and he would teach me anything and everything about astronomy.

Hating the heaviness in my heart that the memories conjure up, I lock them back down and get up. It's a short walk downtown from the house, so I dig a pair of winter boots out of the closet and head out to enjoy the overwhelming holiday spirit.

The snow crunches under my boots, leaving footprints in the powdery snow. The faint sound of singing tickles my eardrums, and I spy a group of carolers outside the Wilsons' house. Through the different frosted windows I pass, Christmas trees glitter brightly, and each house flickers with an array of dazzling lights. I snuggle into my jacket, feeling the warmth the holiday spirit offers.

Willow Falls has always been beautiful. A quaint little town stuck in the middle of nowhere. From the gigantic Easter egg hunt and the turkey races to the Fourth of July potluck and fireworks, holidays are a huge deal here. But nothing tops Christmas.

The town square comes into view, and my heart sings. I may have been in a hurry to get out of this town, but my love of these little things never changes. The beauty in the town square is like no other, from the old historical buildings to the ancient basswood and birch trees. And it's impossible to miss the gigantic Christmas tree with the town's worker bees wrapping it in time for the lighting ceremony tomorrow night. It's one of the biggest events of the season and my favorite time of year. It used to be *our* favorite time of year…

I pass the cafe and barber, both bustling with customers. Each window has a holiday display with frosted snowflakes and mini-Santas. As I walk by the candy shop, I stop to admire the train set. After all these years, I can't believe it's still running. When I make it to the corner of the square, I see the sign for The Trusted Toolbox, my dad's hardware store and smile. A place I spent half my childhood. You can never be too young to learn about bolts and pipes, my dad always said when he had us helping him stock the shelves. I was eager to learn everything about it and made Dad promise he would let me run it when I grew up.

That dream clearly died along with so many others.

The bell rings as I open the door and step inside. The familiar scent of fresh-cut wood, a hint of oil and paint, and freshly cut Christmas trees fill my nose. I brush off the thin layer of snow from my jacket and look around for my parents. A couple stands by the register, debating which saw to choose, while another woman lifts paint samples up to the light. Mr. Clemons, my old gym teacher, walks down the aisle, and I wave at him as I make my way to the back in search of Mom and Dad. I move to push against the double doors, but instead of going inward, they push out.

I stumble backward, and my boot slips. Losing my balance, I reach out for anything to steady me, but all I catch is air. I cuss as I go down.

Two *monster*-sized hands wrap around my waist before I become one with the hard floor. Just as fast as I lost my balance, I'm righted back on my two feet. "Holy, almost brain explosion. Thought I was gonna. . .take out. . ." I don't finish my sentence.

My eyes lift to meet my savior, and a bit of shame washes over me. I can't help but take him in, inch by inch as if he's a piece of meat and I'm fucking starving.

This guy seeps masculinity from his cut shoulders, his lean waist, to his sharp jaw and defined cheekbones. I drink him in like a cold glass of lemonade on a hot summer day. I lick my lips like a feline in heat, taking in the gritty stubble along his jawline, and how his plump lips are formed into a tight smile. *Does God still make specimens this flawless anymore?* I can't remember the last time I saw someone so…so… Jesus, I'm in serious need of *I'm so much better than my ex* sex. It's as if I saved the best for last. His beauteous gaze. Magnetic eyes. If I look too long, he'll forever bewitch me, but it's impossible to pull away. A long, long time ago, in a different life, I consumed those eyes, those full lips.

I inhale a sharp breath as my brain catches up. Gone is the lean, shy boy who kissed me under the pine tree on Wicker Street and snuck into my bedroom every night after my parents went to sleep. Before me is a… is a… beast.

"Liam?" I say his name as if there may be a mistake. There's no way this is. He is…

"Holly." My name is a deep purr off his tongue. God, even his voice is different.

"How—when—how?" I should ask myself why in the world I can't conjure up a damn sentence! "You look so… different." Like a Viking with a chip on his shoulder. And I may be the chip. . .

"Time changes people, Holls."

It sure does.

I knew I would run into him at some point. It was inevitable with him helping at the hardware store. But the first person I see? I don't know whether this is a sign or fate hates me.

"Oh, look! You two found each other!" My mom's voice rings out, slapping me across the face. Realizing we're holding each other like a couple of lovesick kids, I drop my arms like he just caught fire and back away.

"Yep. Just—bam—ran into each other. Or…well, I fell, and—Mom!" I throw myself into her arms, almost knocking her over. "I missed you!" I hug her tight, trying to gather myself, and make the mistake of looking over her shoulder at Liam. His watchful eyes continue to take me in. His magnificent lips are in a thin line. Guess he's still holding a grudge. Pulling my gaze from him and moving away from my mom, I say, "I went home first, and no one was there. I thought you would have been busy baking."

Mom waves her hand and sighs. "That hasn't been a tradition in years. No need to bake cookies for just me and your father."

A pang of guilt ripples through me, her message coming through loud and clear. My brother is gone, and I abandoned them.

I regret my words. Regret looking back at Liam even more. I left him too. He doesn't have to come out and tell me he hates me or still holds my choices over me. It seems even time doesn't mend old wounds.

"I'm sorry. I didn't—you loved baking. I just assumed you always—"

"No worries, honey. Now that you're home, we can bring back some old traditions. Your father wouldn't mind some unhealthy cookin'. You know, his doctor said—"

"My girl! She finally returns!" Dad bellows from the storage room before he even appears. Just the sound of his voice has my throat locking.

"Dad," I whisper, running into his embrace. I snuggle into his burly chest, loving the infinite smell of sawdust.

"Glad you're home, sweet girl. Your mother's been up my rear. Hopefully, you can keep her company while I get some peace and quiet."

I laugh into his chest and pull away, swiping at the wetness under my lids. "Yeah, right. You love it when she nags you. It keeps you on your toes."

"It keeps me insane! You should see what she's feeding me nowadays. Not even the squirrels will eat the leftovers."

"Henry, it's for your own good."

"Woman, if you want what's good for me, cook me a damn steak. Win my heart over again with some starch and a damn pie. Otherwise, I'm gonna be forced to go out searchin' for someone who's gonna feed me the way a man should be fed."

I slap my dad on the shoulder. "Oh, please. You wouldn't survive a day without Mom looking after you." A tender smile breaches my face at the way my parents gaze at one another. True love, forty years in the making. I gaze over at Liam, knowing it's a mistake the second I do. Once upon a time, he looked at me like I was his world. His happily ever after. Now, he looks at me like I'm the villain. A walking bad memory. If we were both honest, it wasn't all on me. He had his faults. He made hurtful decisions too. But I refuse to go down that road again of who hurt who the worst.

Dad speaks up, snapping the live wire of emotions crackling between us. "Well, time is money. I have to get these parts delivered to the Johnsons. Bill's car battery went caput, and his jumper cables are shot, so he needs me to drive it on by. Liam, can you still help in the back while I'm gone? I'm sure Holly can—"

"I… actually, I'm gonna head back home. Something's not agreeing with me." I throw a sharp glance at Liam then turn to Mom. "Wanna maybe get some cookies in the oven? I can really use something sweet right now."

Take that.

Mom smiles and gives Dad a kiss. "Don't be home too late. We're making Holly's favorite tonight."

My eyes light up. "Chicken fried steak with loads of mashed potatoes and homemade gravy?"

"Well, I'm certainly not going to use a pre-made gravy. That's like committing a sin. Everything must be from scratch."

Amen to that. Knowing that's also Liam's favorite, I turn to him while I grab Mom's arm. "Can't wait to eat every. Last. Bite. Won't be a lick leftover." Because I'm a child, I stick my nose up and smile, pulling my mom past him and my dad. Feeling like I just won the annual turkey trot race, I skip out, my mom locked on my side.

Chapter
three

I'm still basking in my win as I set the table for dinner. Liam may hate me. He may even have a right to, but he's not innocent either. We both made choices that night. We both said horrible things. We both walked away. If he thinks he's going to break me down with those searing eyes and new and improved beast-mode body, he has another thing coming.

I put the plates down and adjust the silverware.

Where *did* that body come from anyway? You'd have to be blind not to be affected by him. He's always knocked me off my axis, but now? I should have known it was him the second he touched me. That magnetic attraction had always been too strong between us. Instead of admitting that's why his touch almost set my panties on fire, and he still affects me, I remind myself he's a jerk and said awful things to me and—

"Hey, Mom, you gave me too many plates."

I can count, right? Three people, four plates. Mom sticks her head out of the kitchen. "No, honey, it's right. We have a guest coming for dinner."

The doorbell rings, and my eyes shoot to the front door just as my dad pops up from the basement. "I'll get it."

"Wait!" I spit out, but it's too late. Dad is already opening the door to Liam. I don't hide my scowl as he walks in and hands my dad a bottle of wine.

"If I remember, that's your favorite."

"Any wine is my favorite as long as the wife doesn't take it away. Come on in. Holly was just setting the table. Food is almost ready."

Liam walks in and slides off his jacket. Poor thing can barely fit over his huge muscles. Looking over at me, the kind smile he held for my father slips, and he says, "Oh, good. I'm starved. Can't wait to dig in."

Jerk.

Dinner is a complete bust.

This was supposed to be *my* meal. *My* chicken fried steak and bottomless mashed potatoes. Instead, I have Liam sitting across from me, making pleasant conversation with my parents while he eats *my* meal. I shove a bite of potatoes in my mouth and wash it down with a huge gulp of wine. If he's gonna eat my meal, I'm going to drink *his* wine.

"Margaret, this is your best yet. No one makes fried steak like you do." He takes a hefty bite, and Mom smiles widely, eating up the compliment. I roll my eyes, mocking his stupid compliment under my breath, and take another deep sip of wine.

"What was that, honey?"

"Oh, nothing. Just thinking about the tasty cookies. Especially the brown sugar candy cane ones. Once Liam leaves, I'm gonna dig in." I take another swig.

Liam's gaze locks on mine. Cool as a cucumber, he lifts his glass, slowly bringing it to his lips. Soft, plump, inviting.
. .

I slam my wine.

"Oh Liam, you should stay for dessert. If I remember

right, you used to love those cookies. Holly made an extra batch of them."

Jesus, Mom! "I was going to give them to the homeless." Plus, I poisoned them. Mom gives me a side glance and waves me off, continuing to praise Liam for basically just breathing. *You're such a big help, Liam. You're so this, Liam. You're so that, Liam.*

"Gah!"

Mom jumps in her seat. Apparently, that was *not* said in my head. "Sorry. Bad bite." Bad everything. Coming home was supposed to be healing for me. Getting over all the shit in my life. Not throwing myself into more shit. I startle my mother again when I shove my chair back and stand. "Sorry. I need to make a phone call." Reaching over, I snatch the bottle of wine off the table, turn my back, and head through the kitchen.

I shove my feet into a set of boots and head outside. The crisp chill washes over me, calming my overheated nerves. Who the hell does he think he is? And why is he here? I lean against the garage and take a pull of wine. Am I losing it? The memories I've tried hard to bury are fighting their way to the surface, and the barely healed scars of our past are re-opening. Has it been so long that I'm confusing what really happened that night?

"We had a plan. You're not sticking to the plan."

"We still have a plan. It's just a year or two, Holly. It'll be over before we know it, and we'll be together again. We can do this—"

"No, we can't. Because I won't."

"Still running, I see."

I whip my head to the left. There Liam stands, hands shoved in his pockets, staring at me intently. "Oh, you're one to talk. Speaking of, why don't you just run your pretty little ass out of here."

He takes a step toward me. "That would be rude of me."

I take a swig. "Nah, I'll cover for you. Tell my parents you got explosive diarrhea and had to hurry home. Which is where? Why are you home? Thought you were off saving the world?"

"I'm back."

Wow, still a man of many words.

"Why are you back, Holls? After all this time. Been gone so long, I never thought you would come back. Sounds like you're doing well for yourself. Got everything you ever wanted."

No. All I ever wanted was you.

Shit.

I tap my foot against the garage, my expression pinched. I angle the bottle to my lips and drink until I drain it. Liam's gaze doesn't falter, and I hate the way he looks at me. It's confusing. It hurts. It angers me. "Yeah, guess I did, didn't I?" I push off the wall, hating the lie as it falls off my tongue. I step toward him until our feet touch and strain my neck to keep eye contact. "And what about you? Looks like you've been busy eating small children and growing into a Viking. What's your story? Where's your arm candy this fine evening? Wife? Oh, wait, is she at home with your cute-as-a-button kids?" It pangs me to even think of him happily married with a beautiful wife and any cute-as-a-button kids.

He doesn't answer right away, and my stomach bottoms out. Why did I ask a question I didn't want the answer to? She's probably beautiful and perfect and treats him the way he should have always been treated.

"No wife," he responds, and I shamefully let out a relieved breath.

"Oh. Ye-ah?" my voice cracks, and I have to clear my throat. "Why's that?" *Shut up, Holly.*

"Because I never got over you."

My lips part. My jaw slips, practically slamming against the concrete. He doesn't say another word or stick around for my response. Just turns and disappears back inside.

Chapter
four

T he next day...

The smell of warm apple and cherry pie fills the house while Christmas music croons and crackling firewood sounds from the fireplace. It's officially almost Christmas. Dad is in the living room watching sports while mom and I finish the last batch of pies.

The rest of the night was a total bust. By the time I gathered myself and came back inside, Liam was gone. Mom said he had other engagements, which only made me more agitated. How does one throw a bomb like he did at me and not stick around for me to grill him about it! He's not over me. What does that even mean! And what engagements? Did he really have someone else? That thought sent me into a whirlwind where I drowned my damn jealousy with spiked eggnog.

I barely slept as I tossed and turned, my dreams all leading back to him. The way he looked at me, his hands shamelessly did things to me... Now, I'm in the worst mood ever, lacking sleep, and definitely not feeling very holiday-ish.

I slide the apple cobbler into the oven when the doorbell rings, followed by the yelling of Kelly Anne, my high school best friend.

"Where the hell is she? I mean, heck. Sorry, Mr. Bergner." She follows the smell and finds us in the kitchen. "There she is. Our fancy city girl. Doesn't pick up the phone and bother telling her best friend she's finally comin' home."

What's with everyone hammering on the guilt? She has a right, I suppose. I've been a horrible friend. We've kept in touch throughout the years, but it's always been through text or email. Lots of rain checks and blown-off dates because I was always so busy with my new life. "I'm sorry. It was such a last-minute thing."

"Yeah, yeah, get over here." Laughing, I wipe off my hands and give her the biggest *I'm an ass of a friend, but I missed you, and I'm glad to be back* hug. She looks the same. Her love for bulky sweaters and leggings hasn't died. Her hair is still big and out of control. "Lookin' good, Bergner, but I have to ask, do they not feed you in the big city? You're like a frail little thing."

"I agree. She needs to eat more," Mom pipes up in the background.

"I eat tons. How are you? How's James? Are you two finally—"

"Getting a divorce."

"Oh shit."

"No, no. Don't feel bad. It's for the best. We love each other but not enough to try not to kill one another. It's safer this way." I hug my friend again because you can never have enough friend hugs.

"Well, I'm sorry anyway. But you deserve to be loved and not murdered so. . ."

We both break out into a fit of laughter. The timer on the oven goes off, but Mom waves us off.

"You two go catch up. I'll finish in here."

We head into the living room, where my dad is now

26

fast asleep on the couch. Turning down the television, we share the loveseat.

"Okay, so tell me, how are things with you? Last time I checked, you were up for a fancy promotion and things were heating up with Vincent."

I open my mouth to dish out the truth. How my life is in turmoil. That perfect job is no more. That perfect man is not so fucking perfect. I want to be honest and confide in her. She's been my closest friend since I was in training diapers. But the way she looks at me, so excited to celebrate in my successes…my chest tightens, and the lies start to fall. "Great! It's all great."

Her brow turns upward. "That's it? That's all you're gonna give me? What about Romeo? Any signs he's gonna pop the question? Last time we talked, you said—"

"Yeah, I don't know. It's. . .he's. . ." A cheating, lying, manipulative jerk. "He's just so busy. We both are. We're content with how things are for now."

Her brows shoot up her forehead. I'd react that way too. That answer was horrible. Two stiff, boring people who are content. "Okay. . .well, now we gotta talk about Liam. You know he's back in town, right?"

"Yeah. I know."

"Then you must know he's not the Liam you remember. Like, we're talking man of steel, gritty, always frowning, but looks so hot while doing it that he melts the panties off anyone who walks by him, Liam."

I would have added the word smoldering.

"Yeah, I saw."

Her eyes pop wide. "You did? How? When? What did you do? What did *he* do? Jesus, tell me before I combust—"

"Shhh!" I slap her on the shoulder and peek over at my dad, making sure she didn't wake him with her outburst. "I saw him yesterday at the hardware store. Apparently, he's been helping my dad."

"And?"

"We ran into each other. Literally. I was going into the back at the same time he was coming out. The door knocked me over, and instead of falling ass-first to the floor, he caught me. Before I even realized it was him, I'd licked his whole body in my mind and basically wet my panties, fantasizing about being taken by such a beast. When our eyes finally met, reality hit me like a sledgehammer. I realized I was looking at my ex, who hates me, and I think I should hate him, but before I could tell him how superb he looked and felt, my mom interrupted, and I jumped away like he was a burning building and ran off." I exhale, throwing my back against the couch.

Kelly Anne stares at me, her jaw dropped. I know. A lot to take in. "Wow."

"Yep. But don't worry. It's already been established there's still bad blood. He's clearly still angry. And honestly, I'm not here to lick his wounds. I just want to get through Christmas and get home."

"Aren't you just the least bit curious where he's been?"

"No." I can't even say it with a straight face. "Okay, fine, yes. A million questions are running through my mind. Where has he been all these years? Why is he a tank? Is he with someone? Why is he back home?" *Jesus, Holly, take a breath.* "I don't know. Maybe I don't want to know the answers. Maybe we need to leave the past in the past."

"Hmmm," she hums, joining me against the couch.

Mom pops her head out of the kitchen. "Honey, the pies are done. Can you help me box them? They need to be taken over to the community center for the tree lighting ceremony tonight."

Kelly Anne nudges me as we get up from the couch and go into the kitchen. She whispers, "Remember that one time your mom made us drive all the pies to the community center?"

I start to laugh. "How could I forget?"

"It was epic. Twenty pies slamming against the roof after we hit that pothole."

"We were jamming out to Britney so loud, I missed the construction signs."

Kelly Anne busts out laughing. "Legit spent days cleaning apple cobbler out of my hair."

I saw my life flash before my eyes that day. Mom had been slaving for days making those pies and trusted us to get them there safely. While Kelly Anne ran my car through the car wash, trying to wash away the evidence, I went to the grocery store and spent three months' worth of my allowance buying out their entire bakery.

"Mrs. Bergner, these all look delicious. Need any taste testers? Just in case?"

Mom sets the boxes down and pulls out a warm cherry pie. "If I remember right, you both love cherry."

"Heck yeah!" Kelly Anne boasts, taking the fork Mom hands her. I take one as well, and without shame, we eat the entire damn thing while we box the remainder of the pies.

I groan as I box the last one. "Why did I eat all that?"

"Because it's a sin not to eat a pie your mom makes."

That's not what my stomach's saying right now. "All right, let's get these in the car. I'll drive them over—"

"Oh no, honey. You're off the hook."

"Why? I can take them."

"It's okay. I already have someone coming to deliver them." On cue, the doorbell rings. We both turn and peer through the kitchen and the living room. The door opens, and Liam, looking like a goddamn winter model in a pair of jeans and a black shirt under his winter coat, walks in.

"*Seriously*, Mom?" Dammit, he looks good. Like *sex on a stick*, good. *Better than mom's cherry pie*, good and *that's* good.

"I know better than to let you two handle the pies."

"Wait, what? You knew?"

"Of course I knew." Mom sets her towel on the counter and goes to greet Liam as we trail behind. "Liam, thank you for helping me. You're just too kind."

"Not a problem," Liam replies. I take a peek at him and instantly regret it. My knees wobble. He has yet to take his eyes off me, and I hate how exposed I feel under his gaze. He walks up right in front of me, lifts his hand, and gently brushes his thumb along the corner of my mouth. My chest tightens, restricting my breath.

"Always did have a sweet tooth," he says, retracting his finger, a tiny smear of cherry filling coating his thumb.

Time stops. It's just him and I. Young and naïve. Thinking nothing will ever get in our way. Two kids in love and unstoppable. We were going to run away and live our very own happily ever after.

Until one day, we weren't.

Choices were made. Regrets happened.

And in a blink, our love was a ghost.

I fight my way back from the emotions of the past and wipe at my face. "I actually don't like sweets anymore. I'm a total salt fiend now. Can't get enough."

God, why do I always divert? Why can't I just say, yes, I love sugar? Just like I did when we were kids. When you would sneak me candy bars when I was grounded. When I got my tonsils out, and you spoon-fed me Frosties. When we did that thing with whipped cream while my parents were out at a movie.

Ugh!

Why is he here? Doing all this nice stuff for my family when he's supposed to hate me. Why is he inserting himself back into my life when all he wanted to do was get away from me?

The mood in the room changes. My mind switches from remembering whipped cream on my boobs to the horrid words we spat before he walked out on me. It was the last time I saw him. Until yesterday.

Liam's eyes darken, his mood also changing as the past creeps back in. As if we're having the same thoughts. Silently having the same argument. And in our heads, we're loud and angry.

Mom clearing her throat snaps us out of whatever alternative universe we were trapped in. "We should really get these pies in the car. The tree lighting ceremony starts in a few hours."

I clap my hands together to avoid more interaction with Liam, turn around, and walk into the kitchen. And then I don't stop. I walk right out the back door. Forgoing boots, shoes, and all, I step up onto the ledge of the deck and body dive into a large mound of snow. The second the snow slams into my body, I hiss in agony. Definitely a lot colder than I imagined. But even the sharpness of the cold snow doesn't cool down the burning sensation in my chest.

I should have never come home.

"Are you sure you're okay?" Mom asks me for the millionth time. Why is everyone so worried about me?

"Yes, Mom. Totally fine." Everyone keeps acting like it's not normal to jump in a pile of snow, barely clothed and without shoes. "I'm just tired. I have a lot on my mind. But I'm fine. I promise."

Mom's sigh gets me every time. "I wish you didn't work so hard. Do you miss Vincent? I told you he's welcome to stay with us. Maybe you should call him—"

"No. It's not that. I'll be fine. Let's just drop it and enjoy tonight, okay?" She wants to pry, to ask more, but she holds her tongue and nods. Taking my hand, she walks with me through the town square. Willow Falls starts the Holiday celebration as soon as the dishes are cleared on Thanksgiving, but tonight is the annual tree lighting ceremony. Not a single person misses out. Streets have been blocked off, and food trucks line the sidewalks, serving everything from cotton candy to funnel cakes to any fried food you can think of. Mr. Gibson, our annual Santa, walks around, waving at the littles with his wife, Mrs. Claus, by his side. The carolers are in full effect, singing holiday cheer. Even the most humbug spirit finds warmth and happiness tonight.

My parents get stopped by a neighbor, and I catch Kelly Anne waving at me. I tell them I'll meet up with them before the lighting ceremony.

"Hey! How you doin'?"

"I'm fine. God, why does everyone keep asking me that?"

She puts her hands up in surrender. "Whoa. Just asking. It's not every day someone starts mumbling under their breath like a madwoman, then walks off, and Olympic dives into a sketchy pile of snow. Any chance you already knew it was deep enough that you wouldn't become part of the ground when you took that plunge?"

The freezing cold snow smacking me in the face jump-started my brain, and I ended up just as confused by my actions. "Of course I did. Otherwise, I wouldn't have done it." I definitely did not.

"Hmmm, you look like you did that one time in high school when I asked you if you went down on Liam, and you totally lied because you were too embarrassed to admit it."

"Because I didn't."

"You admitted it three days later—"

"Whatever! Just let's forget that. I already have. Hey, Mr. Garrison still hand out spiked hot cocoa?"

Kelly Anne scoffs. "Duh. It's like his one job during the holidays."

"Good. I need a few."

Ever since I was a little girl, I have loved Christmas. The smells of cinnamon and pine lingering in the air, sugar pouring through the doors of the candy shop. Even Dad's hardware store has the most enticing aroma of maple bourbon potpourri.

I finish the rest of my hot cocoa, loving the little hint of peppermint. The town bells start to ring, signaling the lighting ceremony is about to begin. I look around, searching for my parents, when I'm halted by the sight of Liam. He's standing on the other side of the tree. I try to glance past him, but he captures my attention, holding my gaze. He's blank-faced, showing no emotion, and I can't help but wonder what's made him so cold. The Liam I used to know always smiled. His laughter would make my heart flutter. Now, he seems so jaded. Angry. I assumed it was his hatred toward me, but I think there's more to it. There's a story there, and I'm guessing it's not pretty. I wonder where he's been all these years. Has he thought of me? Does he have regrets like I do?

The first year away from home—away from *him*—was agony. I was living in my own personal hell and knew there was no way I was ever going to crawl out. I missed him. I missed us. I cried myself to sleep for months, wishing I could take back all the horrible things I said. What if we hadn't been so angry that night? I should have fought harder for him to stay. But he should have fought harder not to let me go.

Liam and I were a force. We hadn't just loved each other; we'd owned each other. Our souls had been linked indescribably. I could feel his heartbeat inside me. Hear his every thought. It was something intrinsic and hard to define.

We were going to run away together. Build a house on a hill with a white picket fence. Have our kids and dogs. I was going to open a bakery, and he would become a firefighter or a doctor. We were going to be forever.

"Holls, you gotta hurry."

"Where are we going? The lighting ceremony is about to start. Our parents are gonna be mad if we're not there." *He doesn't answer me, just holds my hand as we rush through the crowd, squeezing through people until we're behind the gigantic tree.* *"Liam—"*

"Shhh…"

He sneaks us past the "Do Not Enter" sign, past the wires and electrical boxes, then tells me to kneel and guides us into the tree. *"Liam, are you insane? We're gonna get electrocuted! They're about to light the. . ."*

He tugs me farther until we're at the center of the Christmas tree. It's been hollowed out. *"Liam, how'd you do this—"*

"Lie down."

"This is in—"

"Just do it."

Pursing my lips, I do as he says. He reaches for my hand, weaving his fingers through mine. The townspeople begin the count-down from beyond the tree. When they hit one, my breath is stolen as the entire tree explodes in the most hypnotizing colors.

"It's. . .beautiful," I whisper, enamored by the scenery. He turns on his side. "We're going to have a life even more beautiful than this. Remember this moment. Hold on to it. One day, it will be ours. . ."

It wasn't a proposal, but it was as close as we got.

A couple months later, my brother, the hero of our family, died. Billy had plans to go to college, get married, and become someone wonderful. He'd brag that he was going to become a doctor or a lawyer offering free legal aid to the less fortunate who don't have the means to get counsel. His dreams were colossal. But so was his heart. He hated seeing the other part of the world suffer. Without thought, he joined the Peace Corps. It was his way of giving back. College was put on hold, and before the news even settled in, he was gone.

His letters barely numbed the pain of his absence. My parents didn't understand his choices, and I was angry at him for leaving me. But while we were suffering with his decision, he was immersing himself in underdeveloped countries, making this world a better place. He promised us he would be back once he made his mark on humanity.

Billy was on a volunteer mission, transporting supplies to a local village when his Humvee was attacked.

He was gone for under a year. He never came home.

My world shattered. It broke my parents.

After that, all of our lives fell apart.

"I remember this being one of our favorite times of the year." I'm pulled from my thoughts, not realizing Liam had moved. He's like a giant next to me. I have to crane my neck to look at him. I wish I could turn off my emotions and not feel this connection. No matter the time lost or mound of regrets, he still owns me.

I clear my throat and stare back off into the crowd. "That time doesn't exist anymore." Mayor Riley starts speaking through the intercom, reciting his annual holiday speech, cutting off further conversation. I smile at my mom when she gets recognition for her pie donation, then my dad when he's mentioned as having donated a portion of the lights for the tree. He continues going through a list of people who contributed until I hear Liam's name.

"And to our very own Liam Cody. We thank you for your service." I gaze at Liam while the town claps. He stares straight and nods his thanks. When the mayor announces it's finally time, the entire town starts the countdown.

Ten. Nine. Eight.

"Tell me you'll do this with me forever."

Seven. Six. Five.

"One day, I'll put the biggest ring on your finger and get you to marry me."

Four. Three. Two.

"Tell me you'll forever be mine, Holls."

One.

The lights flash in the most beautiful array of colors. You can feel the surge of joy as the bright bulbs dazzle onto the smiling faces in the crowd. The choir sings, and everyone holds hands in the first annual town Christmas carol. Liam takes my hand, and I startle, barely registering it when my mom takes my other. He stares down at our hands, then locks his gaze on mine. The kiss we shared under the magical tree. The one that bonded us forever... which wasn't forever at all.

"Tell me you didn't. Tell me you didn't!"

"Holly, please. Hear me out. You can come with me. They do housing for—"

"Stop. I've heard enough."

"You've heard nothing. You're not even listening to me."

He grabs my hand, but I rip it away. "Don't touch me. I can't believe you did this. After everything that's happened. This is selfish."

"How is it selfish? I'm doing what's right—what he would've wanted."

"He would not have wanted you to go over there. He would've wanted you to stay with me." My voice cracks, and I choke back a sob.

His tone is softer when he speaks again. "I'm going to be with you, Holly. It's only for a couple year—"

"It's a suicide mission!" I scream. "He said the same thing, and he never came back! That was his journey—not yours. We have a plan. Our own plan."

He exhales slowly, his mind already made. "And things change. I'm asking for two years."

I shake my head violently as the tears fall. "No, you're asking me to wait behind until I get the same call my mother did."

"You won't."

"You don't know that!"

"I know I would never leave you—"

"But you are! That is exactly what you're doing. You are abandoning our plan to go across the world and fight a battle with no good ending. You're sitting here promising me things you have no right to. Do you think my brother signed up to die? When he waved goodbye to my parents, do you think he knew it would be for the last time? Do you think he knew he was going to get blown to smithereens all because he wanted to help someone? If so, you're foolish. And definitely not the man I thought you were."

My words are harsh, but I'm desperate. Backed up into a corner with no way out. He wants to leave me to fight a losing war. My pleading turns to anger. I spew out threats. It's the only way. He'll *have to choose me. He'll choose us. "I won't be part of this. I won't wait for you, let alone go with you. And don't expect me to see you off. You'll be nothing to me. Because that's clearly all I am if you do this to us."*

My heartrate speeds up. My chest cracks. My breathing becomes rapid. I'm falling apart all over again.

I break away, tearing my hand from his, and turn around, pushing through the crowd. Tears pour down my cheeks as I tug at my jacket for air. I find solace down an alley and hide in the darkness, heaving in deep breaths.

"Holly."

I throw my hand behind me as I almost keel over. "Get away from me." He makes his way deeper into the alley. I whip around. "I said leave. I don't want to see you. I want absolutely nothing to do with you."

"Too bad. Because I think it's about time we hash this out."

"Hash it out? Hash what out?"

"We're both still angry. That's apparent. And I'm done fucking feeling this way. You probably want answers, and damn straight, so do I."

Oh, the nerve. I storm up to him, jabbing my index finger into his chest. "Answers? You're damn straight I want answers. For starters, was it worth it? Throwing everything away for someone else's dream. To break my fucking heart and destroy the only path I knew—the only one I wanted. Was it worth it?"

"That's a selective memory you have, Holls."

"Pretty sure that's exactly what happened."

Liam tucks his hands into his jacket pockets. "Would've never made you give up your dreams. I would've done anything to make you happy. I just asked one thing of you."

I scoff at him. "You asked me to give up our entire life

plan so you could go follow someone else's dreams. My heart broke once, I wasn't going to allow it to break all over again."

"I would have come back to you."

"Billy said the same thing. He didn't. You chose to risk your life and die over choosing me. You made your decision clear that night."

"I asked you to come with me. We could have built a—"

"No we couldn't have! Why would you think I would just leave? Uproot my life for you to follow some insane idea that you needed to join the Peace Corps and save the human race? We had plans. Or maybe I only did. Maybe I was just naive and you had planned on leaving me all along."

Liam's jaw tightens. He pulls a hand from his pocket and points a finger at me. "You knew damn well where I stood. I begged you. You wouldn't listen to a damn thing I said."

"Because my options were to go with you and risk you dying or wait for you with the same possible outcome. I refused to do that."

"And don't I know it." His curt statement hurts. I know damn well he's referring to the letter he left me that night after our fight. Asking me to come with him. If not, to at least see him off and give him the strength in knowing I'll be there when he returned. If I didn't come, my intentions would be clear.

Liam shipped out three days later. And I never showed.

"But I guess it all worked out for you in the end. Instead of coming with me—shit, even waiting—you ran away. Seems I did you a favor. Holls with the perfect life. The perfect job. The perfect man. Turning your back on me gave you everything you wanted."

"Fuck you."

"You ain't mine to fuck anymore, Holls."

I flinch at his words. They cut deep into old wounds I've fought for years to heal. But I refuse to let him break me all over again. My pride won't allow it. I straighten my shoulders, hiding the raw emotions he's threatening to expose and reply in anger. "Damn right, I'm not yours. You gave that right up. And you know what? I *am* living my best life. All the things I've ever wanted are at the tip of my fingers because I wasn't naïve and didn't wait for *you*."

He reaches out and wraps his hand around my neck. I suck in a hard breath as his mouth slams against mine in a bruising kiss. I want to fight back. Push him off. Have him never touch me again. But my body refuses. I lose all sense of reality. My arms go up, and I dig my nails into the back of his neck, clawing at his skin. I kiss him back, punishing him in the same way. Brutal. Painful. Savage. Neither of us holds back as we fight for control. To get closer. Deeper. To fill the hole left inside us five years ago.

He pulls away, pressing kisses to my chin and down my neck, sucking on my flesh. I arch my head back, and a shameless moan falls off my lips as his teeth nip at my skin. It becomes too much. I slide my fingers into his hair and tug, needing his lips back on mine. I kiss him hard, trying to erase the memories. The years I've spent feeling empty inside. The years I've spent trying to create the perfect life. A ruse—a ploy to make myself think I'm happy.

Suddenly, there's a wetness between our lips, and I realize I'm crying. I remember him walking away. His absence. The endless number of times I broke down and begged for my life to be different. To go back and tell him I would wait for him. Just to have a single moment more with him. All the suffering I endured because of his selfishness.

I tear my lips off his and shove out of his embrace. Without thinking, I raise my hand and slap him across his face. His heavy breathing matches the pounding inside my chest. "I don't belong to you anymore. I haven't for a very long time. Leave me alone."

I dart out of the alley and, without a single glance at the most beautiful Christmas tree anyone will ever see, run home.

Chapter
five

"Come on, Holls. Give me an idea."

"No. It takes the fun out of it. You're just going to have to guess."

"If you want me to guess, I'm going to get you a pet hamster."

I laugh, slapping at his chest. "Don't you dare."

"Then give me an idea. I wanna make sure I get you the best Christmas present ever."

"But you already did. You gave me you." I press my lips to his. They're soft. A perfect fit against mine. He scoops me up by the butt, positioning me on his lap, and kisses me back. "My parents are going to be home soon."

"Then we better hurry." He winks and pulls me back in for the most breathtaking kiss.

I stir awake at the memory in my dream. There's a soft knock on my door, and I grumble, turning on my side, wanting to sleep forever.

"Morning, honey. I was wondering if you wanted to go shopping with me today. I still need to get some last-minute gifts and wasn't sure if you needed to pick up any yourself. Or for Vincent."

Vincent.

Strangely, I haven't thought about him since I arrived home. . .since. . .well, I've been too busy pining over my other ex—who I kissed last night—who kissed *me* last night in the most beautiful, devastating way...*just* before I slapped him and ran off.

"Ugh," I grunt.

"Oh, honey, are you not feeling well?"

With my face stuffed in my pillow, I say, "I'm feeling just fine." Embarrassed. Embarrassed. Did I mention embarrassed? Why did I slap him? *Because he hit a nerve.* Oh yeah. Sounds justified. *You asked for it.* Dammit!

"Are you sure? I can't understand you with your mouth in your pillow."

I pull my face away. "Sorry, I was just saying, yes, I would *love* to go shopping. I have a ton of people still on my list."

She claps her hands together. "Great. Be ready in twenty? We don't want to get stuck in the holiday rush." And then she's off, leaving me to wallow in my actions from last night. Maybe I should just go home. Tack on the lies and tell my parents there's a work emergency I have to get back to. Mom would be upset, but she would understand. Then I could avoid ever running into Liam again and addressing that panty-dropping kiss or the immature slap.

Great plan.

I sit up and throw my legs off the bed, scoping out all my things and how fast I can toss them back in my suitcase.

Another knock sounds on my door. "Your father's already off to the hardware store, so it's just us girls today!" Then she's off again.

I throw myself back onto the bed. What am I doing? I can't leave my mom high and dry. "Can't wait!" I call out, hating myself for even thinking of leaving. God! I'm the worst daughter ever.

I put my ass into gear, sliding into a pair of leggings

and a puffy red sweater. I used to live for Christmas. Liam and I both did. Everything around this time was always perfect in our little bubble. And magical. And then the bubble burst.

After Liam and I went our separate ways, and without much explanation to my parents, I packed my bags and took off. I enrolled in a small institution in the city and pushed myself so hard that I never slowed down enough to allow myself to think of him. I graduated in three years. During that time, I landed an internship at a small advertising company, where I worked my tail off until I was hired full-time.

As the years passed, I moved up in status. Nicer apartments, prestigious social circles. And sometime during the mayhem of my life, I met Vincent. He was that tall drink of water people talk about. He had the looks, the money, and enough brains for me to fall into his bed one night after too many martinis at a work event. I'm not even sure we discussed dating. It just happened. Our lives started to meld, and before we knew it, I was paying rent at one place while living at his. There's no sweep-me-off-my-feet story. No Romeo that kept me there. He was... comfortable. I loved him, obviously, since I spent thirty days sulking on a couch watching pathetic love stories while eating my weight in donuts. But was it the relationship I was mourning? Was it the job? Or was it the fact that I lost two things I had poured myself into so I wouldn't focus on the one thing that truly rattled my soul:

Him.

Still in a fog, I head downstairs, shove my feet in my boots, slide on my snuggly jacket, and find my mom waiting at the door.

The department store is absolutely bananas. Last-minute shoppers are frantic to grab anything they can get their hands on. I stare off into the distance as two ladies fight over a cardigan.

"Honey, do you think your father would like this?" she asks, holding up a flannel jacket he has in every color.

"No, I think he'd love it."

I wander aimlessly through the section of fancy dresses and into the workout clothes. By the time I come out of my daze, I'm in the menswear section, specifically by the Henley shirts. I stop at a gray knit Henley similar to the one Liam had on at the hardware store. I run the fabric through my fingers, remembering the day at the hardware store and how it felt against my skin when my arms were wrapped around him. An earthy scent lingered, and the shirt fit his muscles like a glove. Before I know it, I'm grabbing one in each color.

"Oh, those are great. I'm sure Vincent will love them."

I blink. "Huh?" I stare at my mom.

"The shirts. I assume they're for Vincent?"

I look down, not realizing I have five shirts in my hand. "Oh, uh. . .yeah."

"Well, we better get in line. It's already wrapped around to cosmetics."

As I stand there with my hands full of shirts, I wonder if the kiss affected Liam as much as me. He had to be. What if it was payback, and he just wanted to get me all worked up, then leave me high and dry like I did that day? "Mom?"

"Yes, honey?"

"Do you think. . .okay, say two people used to like each other. Like, *really* like each other, but something happened, and they didn't anymore. Well, one does, but they were too afraid to admit it. Then they see each other again, and it feels like no time has passed at all, but it did because they both made bad decisions and—"

"Holly, I'm sorry. I'm not following."

Shit. What was I saying? "Oh, nothing. It's. . .nothing."
I'm just losing my mind. Kissing my ex, then slapping him,
then buying him a new wardrobe. Don't mind me. The
line moves, and I take a few steps up. *When did I become so
crazy?* Don't answer that, self.

What I do know is I owe Liam an apology. Whether or
not we see eye to eye, I never should have slapped him. I
have to make it right.

"Hey, Mom, I actually need to go. There's something I
need to do." I shove the shirts onto a nearby rack and take
off, halting moments later to turn back. "Any chance you
know where Liam lives? Asking for a friend, of course."

I've never been a picky eater, but I have to say eating crow
is not a favorite of mine. To be honest I would not recom-
mend it. Standing outside Liam's door, I raise my hand to
knock but decide against it. Every few seconds I regain my
confidence and attempt another knock. While I stand there
doing arm work outs, as my hand goes up and down, his
neighbor comes home. I wave, still not trying to make
myself known. "Great day. Love the doormat." He eyes me
warily and hurries into his place.

"Come on. Just do it. Knock, say sorry, and be on your
merry way." Inhale. Exhale. Maybe I should do this
another time. Send an email. Text message? The cool kids
are really into Snapchat nowadays—shit! My hand takes
control of the situation and shoots out, knocking on his
door.

"Why would you do that? I'm not ready!" I hiss to myself.
The door opens, and I straighten, hopefully not looking like
I'm talking to myself like a crazy person. "Hey! Howdy! Jesus,

what are you. . .not wearing?" I slap my hand over my eyes. Liam stands in the doorway in nothing but a pair of sweatpants. Not baggy at all sweatpants. I spread two fingers, shamefully peeking. Abs. So many abs. And…an array of tattoos just over his right peck spreading along his shoulder blade. So many designs over his muscles, so much muscle—shit, I'm staring. "I'm, uh… I'm, uh. . .clearly broken. Looks like I caught you at a bad time. Probably have guests. One who doesn't take swings at you. Well! Okay, I'm gonna just—"

"You coming in or not?"

I'm not sure it's safe. "Can….can you maybe put some more clothes on?" Did I just say that out loud? Tell me I didn't say that out loud.

"You did."

Dammit! Shut up, Holly.

He steps aside, and I nod, clearing my throat, and walk in. I take in his small apartment. Minimal furniture. A television and kitchen table. A miniature, sad looking Christmas tree in the corner. "Nice place."

"Does the job," he says as he grabs a shirt that's on the back of his couch and tosses it over his head.

"Yeah. Hard to snag good property around these parts. High demand—I'm sorry for slapping you." There. I said it. Not sure the babbling beforehand was necessary, but it's out. The problem is, he says nothing back. So, I ramble some more. "And, well. I just. . .it was wrong of me. We shared a nice kiss—more than nice. Explosive. Not to feed your ego, but you've definitely been working on your kissing game since the last time I kissed you. Which, actually, I don't want to know about, because, well, yeah. So, just, sorry. I would like to start over. Wanna go grab some beers?"

Or open your window and throw me out of it?

"Sure."

I wonder how steep the drop would be if he—"Wait, what?"

"I said sure. Gunther's Bar and Grill is just next door. You can buy."

I stand there, waiting for my brain to catch up, as Liam swaps out his sweats and shirt for a pair of jeans and another Henley, then escorts us to the restaurant next door since I'm still in glitch mode. It takes a whole drink before I'm back to myself again.

"So, sorry again. And sorry for what happened back at your apartment." We're seated at a table tucked away in the corner of the bar.

"We both have done things we regret."

"I know, but—"

"Holls, you don't owe me an apology. Let's just call a truce. Let the past be the past. Not sure how long you're here, so maybe we can just enjoy each other's company. Friends?"

Suddenly, I'm staring back at a young Liam, barely a teenager, the first time he said those words to me.

"Look out!"

I don't have time to do that before a gigantic snowball bashes into me. The icy shards explode across my face, and I inhale chilled air. I stand frozen, then slowly raise my hand and wipe away the snow so I can see who I'm about to murder.

"Hey, sorry, I meant to hit my buddy. You kind of came out of nowhere."

"Nowhere?" I hiss. "I was walking in clear sight down the sidewalk."

"Yeah, but in my defense, you're dressed in all white. You kind of blend into the snow."

Oh, the nerve! He's gonna pay. I bend down, scoop a pile of snow into my gloves, and compact it into the perfect snowball. When I lift my eyes, the boy's brows are up, and he's looking back with a humorous smile.

"What are you going to do with that?"

"I'm gonna bring it home and name it as my new pet. What, do you think I'm going to do with it?"

"I was just asking—"

Having a brother taught me to take no prisoners. He opens his mouth, and I fire, hitting him smack in the face.

"Shit! That's cold!"

"Don't I know it." With wide eyes, he suddenly bursts out in laughter. He walks up to me, and I throw up my guard, ready for another fight. He's the same size as my brother. I can jump on his back and take him down.

"I deserved that." He trudges through the snow until he's within close range. I inhale a sharp breath as I get a better look at him.

He sticks his hand out. "How about a truce?"

"Truce." I shake his hand.

"Liam."

Liam, the most beautiful boy I've ever seen.

"Uh. . .Holly."

"Let's start over, Holly. Friends?"

We spent that Christmas becoming friends. Being entranced by one another. Learning everything we could until there was no territory unsearched. And the night of our first tree lighting ceremony, he kissed me.

I blink, bringing myself back to the present. Liam stares intently at me, waiting for my response. I raise my glass. "Truce. Friends it is." Our glasses clink, and I bring mine to my lips. I gaze over my glass at him as we fall silent for a moment, maybe both trying to figure out the rulebook on just being friends. It feels like a lifetime ago since we were just that.

"This place hasn't changed a bit," he starts, breaking the ice. I glance around the bar. Not a single thing has changed since we were kids.

"Tell me about it. Mr. Higsby is even on the same stool." We both peek over at Mr. Higsby, hunkered over his beer, and laughter falls from our lips.

"Billy and I used to come here all the time. We were obsessed with their wings. He taught me how to play pool on those tables. Planned on having our first beers here. He really loved this place."

My playful smile slowly fades. "Yeah. He did." I take another sip of my beer, pushing the emotion back.

"Hey, sorry. I didn't mean to upset you. It's just. . .this place brings back great memories. And I'd like to remember those."

"I just hate that it's all we have left of him."

Liam reaches over and cups his hand over mine. The simple gesture sparks that old flame, and a ripple of heat runs through me. I lift my lashes to meet his. *Friends. Friends. Friends.* I pull my hand away, taking another gulp of my beer. "Okay! Looks like we should probably get another pitcher." I stand, knocking my knee into the table.

A grin tugs at his lips, and he sits back casually in his chair. "Sit down, Holls."

"What?"

"Listen, I get it. This is awkward. The two of us sitting here, trying to be friends. But I'd like to try. We can keep it light. No heavy topics. Simple shit. You start feeling uncomfortable, we drink. It will be our sign to change the subject."

He waits for me to reply. I nod my head slowly, and he

waves over to Hank, the owner of Gunther's, for another round. "I'll go first. How's work? I hear you've really—"

I chug my beer.

He raises a brow. "Okay then, how's city life? Heard—"

I put my empty glass down and grab his to chug.

A laugh barks out of his throat. "Okay, your favorite color still purple?"

I finish his beer, putting his empty mug next to mine. "It is. Thanks for asking. And yours? Still green?"

"It is," he chuckles, refilling our glasses and hiding his laugher by taking a drink.

The next few questions are comical. Favorite foods, TV shows, last book we read. It becomes effortless because we both already know most of the answers. Just like this place, it seems a lot of things never change. We go through a pitcher and play a round of pool. I beat him, but I know he lets me win.

"Okay, my turn." I sit back in my chair. The tension level is at zero, and the beer is giving me a loose tongue. "And you have to be honest."

"Okay." His chest rumbles.

"Do you eat small children for breakfast?"

His brows shoot up, and a beautiful laugh falls from his mouth. "What?"

"Come on! You're huge. Like beast huge. Viking huge. The last time I saw you, you were kind of scrawny. Now, you're like. . .meow—" I slap my hand over my mouth, and Liam throws his head back in amusement at my blunder. "I meant that in a friend way, of course. Friends compliment friends. It's a thing."

"Right. Friends." We hold each other's gaze, feeling like anything but friends.

Liam goes to refill my glass when I blurt out, "Where

have you been all this time?" His hand jolts, and beer splashes outside my mug. It's quick, the subtle change, then it's gone just as fast. He sits down and takes a drink. "What I meant to ask was where has the time gone! Man, my parents are probably wondering where—"

"Are you happy, Holly?"

His question has me tongue-tied. The playfulness in the air shifts. He stares at me intensely, searching for truth. I chicken out and take a sip. He slides his fingers though his hair. "Tell me what you're thinking about right now?" *My body is on fire, and I don't know if I can be just friends. But I'm not sure we can relive the past. We're both damaged. We hurt each other in a way I'm not sure we can get over. I've never stopped loving you.* Another sip. "Have you thought about us?" *Every single day since we walked away from one another.* Another sip.

So much for keeping it lighthearted. My heart is trying to break through my chest. I shoot up. "I need to use the washroom." Without making eye contact, I hurry away.

"Breathe," I mumble to myself. "One foot in front of the other." Why did he have to go there? Ask me those questions? The answers are safe inside my heart. But if I said them out loud, I couldn't take them back. And will him knowing how much I've missed him make it better? Will he feel justified knowing I've ached for him for years? And why did he have to come back looking so freaking hot?

I make it to the bathroom door, but before I push the door open, a hand braces on my shoulder, and I'm spun around. Liam, looking big, bad, and delicious, presses me up against the wall. "I need you to answer me one question."

"Wh-What?" I can't even hide how turned on I suddenly am with him so close to me.

"Is this really what you want? To be friends?"

"I—I don't know what you mean." I know exactly what he means. The way my body is trembling under his touch. The way I can't fight it and suck in my bottom lip. I don't think there was ever a day in my life that I ever just wanted to be friends with Liam Cody.

"Let me break it down for you. You may be locked lip on certain things, but your body language doesn't lie. That dazed look in your eyes. You're making it real hard to be just friends."

My cheeks feel on fire. The ground below my feet is shaking at the anticipation of having him again. "I'm not sure what look you're referring to... I was just..." I can't even filter out a lie, my voice is dripping with arousal.

"Let me refresh your memory. That one time after football practice...you couldn't even hide how turned on you were when I walked off the field. We had sex in my car in the parking lot. On our way to our sophomore dance, you made me pull over, and I tossed you in the back seat and ate you out. Almost missed the dance. How about the movies? We were in the last row, and no one was paying attention when you slipped on my lap and rode me—"

"These are all very fuzzy times. I don't really remember—"

"How about that one time we fucked so hard against the wall in your living room, we accidentally knocked over the Christmas tree."

"We did? Hmmm...don't really—"

"I tried to catch it, but you threatened to cut off my balls if I stopped."

I wipe at the sweat building on my neck. "Sure that was me?"

"As the tree crashed to the ground, your sweet little cunt gripped my cock so hard, and you dug your nails so deep into my back, I still have scars. But man, was it worth it. The way you looked…the way you sounded when you screamed my name—"

"Oh, shut up." My spider monkey arms and legs wrap around him, and I smash my mouth over his. I kiss him hard, deep, forgoing the gentle work-up. He may have been taunting me, but by the feel of the monster pressed against me, he's in just as much trouble as I am.

"For the record, I screamed Holy Mother of God." I grind into him, and we both moan at the friction. He pushes me farther up the wall, his hardness rubbing against my sex.

"Oh *god*," I moan and pull at his hair. How pathetic. I'm two more dry humps away from orgasming.

"What is this, high school? Get a room."

The sound of Mr. Higsby's voice as he walks into the men's bathroom snaps us out of our haze. We're still in the bar. In a hallway. In public.

We both speak at once.

"My place."

"Your place."

He doesn't even bother putting me down. He walks us down the hallway to the back exit and kicks it open. Twenty more feet, and we're at his building. He's a caveman running with me up the stairs, two at a time. If I weren't so turned on already, I'd combust at how incredibly sexy he is. Strong. Determined. Still a damn good kisser.

"You're fucking trembling. You always tremble when you're at your peak."

"Don't flatter yourself. It's just cold." I shut him back up, stealing his breath and pressing my tongue between his lips. He growls and kicks open his door, slamming it closed with the back of his shoe. I don't even have time to prepare before I'm tossed onto his bed.

My hair falls in waves around me as I gaze up at the

most beautiful man I've ever known. I bite down on my lower lip. He looks feral. A man starved and ready to take exactly what belongs to him.

I suck in a breath as he crawls onto the bed, blanketing me with his hard body. His lips drop to mine, and unlike before, they're gentle, more sensual. He unbuttons the top of my jeans, grazing his thick fingers just below my navel. He sucks my lower lip into his mouth, and I moan out in pleasure when his hand disappears inside of my jeans.

"Some things never change. Always so fucking wet for me." He grazes his finger along my slit, teasing me, then spreads me like a flower and slips inside. My fingers latch onto his hair. He pulls out and pumps back into me, each thrust painfully slow. I raise my hips, silently begging for more, but he doesn't bite.

"Come on, don't be mean."

Liam chuckles against my lips. "You have no idea how mean I can be. You're lucky I've been craving this moment just as bad." He glides out and thrusts back in.

"Shit," I hiss. "Then maybe you should show me. Get on with it—*fuck*. . ." I almost bite my tongue. My head arches back as he powers two fingers in, each time harder, deeper. His eyes darken as my body starts quaking under him. I cry out a breathless moan as my orgasm slices through me.

Liam's fingers disappear, and he raises them to his lips, sucking them into his mouth. "Still sugary sweet."

All control gone, we claw at each other's clothes. He rips my jeans off, and I fumble with his. His shirt is over his head. My sweater over mine. Liam pushes down his pants, taking his boxer briefs with him, and releases his monster cock. "Well, *he's* not how I remember him," I comment, bright-eyed and curious about how that's going to work out for my poor, under-used vagina.

"He's exactly the way you remember. Hungry for you." He reaches into his nightstand then slides a condom over his thick cock. My body trembles as he spreads my legs, opening me to him. His jaw tightens as he eases into me, his eyes locked on mine, and it feels like two universes collide. Everything around us burns to ash as our passion sets fire. The ground below us shakes. Or maybe it's just the sputtering of our hearts. But this connection. The way he feels inside me. As if we're both home. It's indescribable.

He moves, his arms cradling my face, his fingers threading into my hair. His muscles tense as he pulls out, trying to go slow, but it's impossible. The need to become one is too powerful. He powers back in, and my eyesight blurs. I suck in a sharp breath, a rush of adrenaline spiking my desire. Liam is becoming just as lost. He slams into me with the desperation of a man needing to claim me. My hands scrape down his back, my nails leaving their mark. Liam grunts furiously. Dipping his mouth to my breast, he bites at my hardened nipple, and I cry out, wrapping my legs tighter around his waist.

"Fuck, you're so wet and tight." My eyes water at the intensity of each thrust, the edge of another orgasm building. Liam releases and treats my other breast to the same beautiful torture. My back arches, pressing my swollen nipple into his mouth.

"Liam, please. . ." I beg.

"Always so damn greedy. My favorite part about you." Like a wild bull, he gives me exactly what I crave, plunging deep into my throbbing pussy. My walls tighten around him, and I cry out. My orgasm comes in such violent waves, it steals my breath. I fall back against the mattress, and Liam bucks into me one last time before growling my name as he pulses inside me.

Liam falls to the side, holding his chest as he heaves for a steady breath. When our pounding hearts labor, the uncomfortableness settles in. Was this a mistake? Did we just cross a line we shouldn't have? Then Liam breaks the silence.

"Think we're gonna get in trouble for not paying our tab?"

I stifle a smile and turn onto my side. It's the first time I've seen him smile, genuinely smile, since we've reunited. He's wearing the most handsome, devilish grin. I want to jump on top of him and steal it as my own. Kiss it so it's mine. "Already? I know you were always jonesing for it but —ouch!" He lets out a laugh.

"No, I don't want it again. I actually may need a few more minutes."

He holds his chest as he laughs. "Some things sure don't change. Always have been insatiable."

I lift my shoulders in a playful shrug and surprise him when I jump up and straddle him. "And you're still such a drama queen. Always complaining. If you're not interested, just lay back, and I'll do all the work. I'm not against using you for your body. No talking. Just pure—"

I squeal as my back suddenly hits the mattress. He stares down at me with those dark eyes. "Oh, there's no need to use me. I'm more than willing to play along. Just hope you can keep up. Now, don't you dare move," he demands and jumps off the bed. He discards the used condom and fits himself with a new one. Just as quickly, he's back on top spreading my thighs, filling me with his very hard and very willing cock.

Chapter
six

I wonder if this is how it feels to be dead.

No feeling in my legs or arms. The only reason I know I'm still alive is the throbbing of my bruised and bitten nipples. Oh yeah, and my vagina. She's out of commission for a while.

I think I passed out because when I open my eyes, I'm lying on my stomach, still naked. Every part of my body is sore. Moaning, I lift my head and turn to see Liam fast asleep next to me. He's on his back, the bedsheet resting just above his navel. I bask in the beauty of his muscled chest, not a single ounce of fat on him. Seriously, how does one become so flawless? I work my way up from his delicious abs to his chest. My eyes gaze over his tattoos trying to dissect them all. My fingers graze over the two doves over his peck, when my eyes transfix on the design in the center. I pull in a tight breath. How. . .how could I have missed that? Without thinking, I raise my hand and brush my fingers over the ink

"I thought you would need a bit more recovery time than that?" Liam's voice is groggy as he slowly opens his eyes.

"When did you get this?"

He looks up at me, holding my gaze. "Two years after I left."

"Why?" I can't hide the emotion in my voice. I pull my eyes back to his chest where my initials are engraved in the middle of two doves.

"Does it matter?"

"Yes, it fucking matters!" My tone becomes shrill. Why would he do that? His eyes are still fixed on mine. I see the uncertainty. Whatever he will say is going to hurt. He knows it. His apprehension gives him away. "Please…" I ask, calmer this time.

He reaches out, brushing the back of his knuckles along my cheek. "I'd completed my two years with the Peace Corps without a scratch on me, like I promised. My next step was to come home. But when it was time, I realized I had nothing to go home to. You were gone." My eyes pool with tears as I chew on the inside of my cheek. "I lost myself for a bit. Drank heavily. I was hurting. I missed you. My heart was fucking bleeding without you." He pauses while I tease my fingers over his ink.

"One night, I found myself at a tattoo shop. The only thing that made sense to me was you. So, I got two doves over my heart because they symbolize eternal love…and your initials in the center. No matter what happened, no matter the distance or space or end, you'd always own it. Next day, instead of coming home, I enlisted in the military. Powered through basic training. Since I had the Peace Corps under my belt, they allowed me to commit to a three-year term."

Tears race down my face. I release a choked breath and turn to get up, but Liam grabs my arm and pulls me back. "No, you don't get to do that."

"I just need a moment."

"You don't get that either. You asked. I told you. I won't feel bad about it. It's the truth. It's life. You don't get to run from it." He cups my cheek. "Can I show you something?" His thumb strokes my cheek, waiting for a reply.

"Sure."

When he gets out of bed and walks over to his dresser, I can't help but admire his tight tush. He pulls out a stack of papers and brings them back into bed.

"What are these?" I ask as he searches for one and hands it to me.

"It's why I did what I did."

I look down at the piece of paper he hands me. It's a letter. "Is this. . .from Billy?" I'd recognize my brother's handwriting anywhere.

"It is. He sent it to me a couple months after he left."

I look at him, and he nods, giving me permission to read it.

Liam –

Hope this letter makes it to you. I promised you I would write, so you knew I was still alive. Feel like a damn pussy writing you. Next I'm gonna put hearts and kisses. Man, I need to get a girl the second I get home.

Things are crazy here. More intense than I expected. It's taking me some time to adjust. I haven't been here long, but I've already seen some fucked up shit. Stuff I could never tell my parents or Holls. But in the chaos, there's some good coming out of this.

I don't know how to explain it. There are so many kids here. No roof over their heads or proper meals. Wish I could do more, but we're low on resources, and I can only do so much.

Met this little boy yesterday. He can't be older than five or six. I can see his fucking bones. I've been bringing him half of my meals so he gets some meat on him. And you know what he does? He takes it back to his little hut and feeds it to his younger siblings. A fucking five-year-old being the caretaker. How fucked up is that?

I'm going to try to see what I can do to get some more supplies. More food. These kids are starving. God knows he's just one of many.

Running out of room in this happy love letter. Give my sister a hug for me. Tell her I miss the living shit out of her. Hope she's doing okay. Your ass better be taking good care of her, or I'm gonna beat it. Kidding. I trust you like a brother. Watch over her. She needs you right now.

Write more when I can.

Love, your boyfriend,

Billy

I can barely read his signature through my tears.

"The letters go on and on. The malnutrition of the kids. Starving families, dying left and right. His team could only do so much. While Billy was there, he never stopped pushing to get more supplies to civilians. He wrote to the US Agency for International Development about the conditions and how they need to supply some grants to bring in food and clean water. Medicine and clothes. They had none of this. A few weeks before he died, his request was granted. He wrote to me, telling me all the things he planned on doing."

Liam shuffles through the letters and hands me one dated two weeks before he died.

Liam –

Merry Christmas, honey! Man, I miss the holidays in Willow Falls. You all getting Mr. Garrison to secretly hook you up with his hot cocoa? How's my sister? Tell her I miss her, but don't make her cry. Hate for you to have to deal with the fallout. They don't really celebrate Christmas here, unless you consider holiday cards posted to cots celebrating. But I have some news worth celebrating. I finally got a reply back from the head of the Peace Corps. They looked into my request for more supplies and funding. This means, in the next year, I'll supply food to kids in need. Clothes, school supplies. These kids will have the chance to see their fifth, tenth, twentieth birthdays. Because someone is giving them a chance. Once the supplies come in, it's going to take about a year until completion. It's gonna put me past my tour, and Mom is gonna be pissed. But I have to do this. For them. They have no one else. I came here to change lives, and that's what I plan on doing. This place and what the Corps does is amazing. Wish you could experience it with me.

Well, enough about me. Hope you all had a great Christmas. Better have spoiled my sister. She deserves it. Miss you, bro. When I get home, we're hitting up Gunther's for bottomless wings. Your treat.

Xoxox,
Billy

"This. . ." I choke on my words. "This is why you went?"

He nods. "To finish what he started."

I don't know how to take it in. He told me he was leaving. But I refused to listen to anything other than he was leaving me. I only thought about myself. How he was being selfish and not considering my feelings. He was putting both our feelings on hold to give my brother his dying wish.

"I. . .I can't—I need a minute—"

"Oh, no, you don't." He snatches me up before I escape. Before I can hide away and surrender to my grief.

"Please, let me go." He pulls me to him, resting my head against his chest as the dam breaks. I fall apart, and the tears pour down my cheeks. My grief comes in waves, stealing my breath as I choke down my sobs. Liam cradles me in his arms. "I never asked. I never cared to ask why. I just thought of myself. How I felt. I never asked why you—"

"Shhh. . .it wouldn't have changed anything."

I rip out of his arms. "It would have changed *everything.*"

"Would it have, though? Would you have said yes to coming with me? Yes to waiting for me? Yes to years of worrying I would end up like your brother? I still left you. I chose to walk away."

"For him. You did it for him." My chest burns with disgust. This whole time, I was the selfish one. Old wounds burst open, channeling the emptiness I've felt since Billy died. "God, I miss him. I miss him so much."

"I miss him too. Every fucking day." Liam slides his hands under my arms and lays me on the bed, kissing away the tears that fall on my cheeks. He trails down my neck to the center of my chest, using his tongue to massage a perked nipple. I gasp on a sob when his lips continue to graze down past my navel and cover my mound. Two hands clasp my thighs, and he opens me wide, licking at my slick heat.

"Liam," I whisper in a plea. I exhale a staggered moan as his tongue works itself inside me. In and out, it causes me to lose all sense. I slowly forget the pain burning inside me, letting pleasure take over. My hips move as I ride his mouth. Another choppy moan escapes when he adds a thick finger. "Yes, yes. . ." I pant, needing more. "Please don't stop. Don't ever stop. Don't ever leave me." I'm too lost to acknowledge the pleas that fall from my tongue. He inserts a second finger and thrusts deep inside me. My body shakes.

He doesn't show me any mercy as he works his fingers harder. My hips buck under him, but he holds me down, forcing me to take the pleasure he's granting me. "Liam," I whimper his name as I come undone, my body shattering before collapsing. He reaches for a condom, ripping open the package with his teeth and strokes it down his throbbing erection. Aligning himself at my sex, he pushes inside me. I grip his shoulders, holding his chest close to mine.

"I've got you, Holls. I always have. I always fucking

will." He fucks me purposefully. Making a statement. A vow. Telling me I'm his, and he's mine.

We come together, both names falling off our lips. When we collapse against one another, he tucks me to his side. "Sleep. You need it. We'll figure it out in the morning."

Too spent to delve into everything we need to figure out, I close my eyes and find sleep within seconds.

Chapter
seven

I got lucky this morning when I snuck into the house, trying to dodge my parents. Nothing like explaining where you've been and why you look like you've been tossed around like a rag doll all night—especially when you told them you were sleeping at Kelly Anne's. Awkward!

Thankfully, they were already at the store.

Showered and looking less ravaged, I'm on mission number two of sneaking into the store without bringing attention to myself. I open the door slowly, cringing when the bell goes off. "Jingle Bells" blares from the speakers, and I blow out a quick breath. In the clear. When no one pops out of the backroom, I ditch my jacket behind the register, run down an aisle, and throw myself at a shelf, pretending to organize—

"There you are, honey."

"Gah!" I jump three feet at the sound of my mom's voice. "Jesus almighty. A little warning next time. You scared the crap out of me!"

"I'm sorry. How long have you been here? I thought you were coming this morning?"

I shrug, looking at my wrist where I'm *not* wearing a watch. "Oh, I don't know, a few hours. I've been organizing. Some of these containers. Super messy."

Dad and Liam walk up from the back, and I fight the

blush creeping up my cheeks as our eyes lock. Liam stifles a smile, and I have to look away.

Mom sighs. "Oh, you should have come and found me. How was your sleepover with Kelly Anne? I bet it was nice to catch up."

I make another mistake and glance back at Liam, who's trying to conceal another laugh. I feel the heat rising in my cheeks. "It was okay. Boring, actually."

Liam lets out a loud bellow, grabbing my mom's attention. "Boring? You two used to go on for hours chatting. I mean, it's clear you got no sleep. Maybe you should go home and rest. You look a little. . .tired."

Liam walks past me, carrying an armful of boxes. "I think you look beautiful," he whispers under his breath, following my dad out to the delivery truck. Mom pats me on the back and disappears down an aisle.

Alrighty then.

As I'm reaching to put a box of washers on the second shelf, Liam and Dad get back from their delivery.

"Hey, honey."

"Hey, Dad." Looking over my shoulder, I smile at my dad before gazing over to Liam. My lips curl into a shy smile, no doubt causing my cheeks to flush.

"Holly," Liam says in that deep purr. I fumble the box, almost dropping it.

"Liam," I return, loving the way his lips curl into a playful smile. I can't hide mine as I turn back to the shelf in another attempt to place the box.

Heat radiates against my back when Liam steps behind me. "Let me help you with that." I don't reply. I'm not sure I can without giving my dad a show.

"You kids got the rest of the restocking? I need to head up front and handle the register for a bit."

"Got it, Dad," I reply too quickly, hoping my voice sounds calmer than I feel. The second the doors flap shut, Liam twists me around, and our lips fuse. My arms are around his neck as he presses me into the shelf, knocking over a box of filters. Like two teenage kids, we claw at each other, unable to get close enough. His tongue breaches my lips, and I moan into his mouth.

"Love your fucking mouth," he hums, kissing me deeper. He boosts me up by my butt and pushes me back up against the shelf as I wrap my legs around him. Two more boxes fall.

"I love this new and improved Liam. Eating small children really pays off."

His chuckle vibrates against my lips. "When we get out of here, I'm gonna eat your sweet pussy—"

"Holly?"

At the sound of my mom's voice, Liam releases me, and I drop to the ground, tugging my shirt down just as she pops her head in. "That's where the filters go." I bend down, picking up a fallen box. Liam turns his back to my mom, hiding the bulge in his jeans.

"Honey, come up front. Mrs. Powers is here, and she would love to say hello."

"Sure thing!" I say, holding the box upside down. I stand there staring at my mom. "Oh, like, right now? Yep. Put these back. Thanks." I shove the box at Liam and follow after my mom.

Mrs. Powers, my old music teacher, waves at me. "Hello, dear. It's been too long."

"It has," I say, going in for an awkward hug. "How have you been? Still beating kids with recorders?" *What?* I squint my eyes closed. "I mean, teaching kids the recorder? Sorry, I haven't eaten lunch yet. Starved cells."

Ever since I can remember, Mrs. Powers has been known as the mean old woman who would use the recorder to slap people's hands if they weren't on cue.

"Sadly, no. I retired last year. There's a young man teaching there now. Not sure he knows what he's doing." She looks over my shoulder, her eyes lighting up. "Why is that Liam Cody?"

Liam steps next to me and shakes her hand. "Nice to see you, Mrs. Powers."

"Oh, please. Call me Patricia." Seriously? *Patricia*? Ew! "Please tell me you'll be attending the Winter Wonderland Festival at the town square tonight. I volunteered to coordinate The Nutcracker play for the elementary school. It's going to be lovely. It would be great for them to meet a local hero—a soldier who defended our country."

"Wouldn't miss it," Liam says.

Getting jealous of my freakin' seventy-year-old music teacher, I cut in. "Well, okay then. My mom can check you out if you're ready—"

"And you, dear, your mother won't stop bragging about you."

"Oh, wow. That's so nice of—"

"A high-profile job? Please do share."

Dammit. I should have let her flirt with him. "Yep, it's great. Now, if you—"

"You must have some amazing stories to share. Small town girl making it big in the city." My palms sweat, and I wipe them down my jeans. My mouth is suddenly dry, and I lick my lips. I can sense Liam watching me, waiting as well.

I clear my throat. "Honestly, there's nothing to tell."

She waves me off. "Oh, don't be so modest. What was

the job title your mother told—?"

"Honestly, nothing. It's—"

"And please tell us about this—"

Panic shoots up my spine. My belly clenches at the looming question. I'm about to jump at her to shut her up when Liam senses my pending freak-out and saves me. "Mrs. Powers, how about I check you out?"

My mom presses the back of her hand to my forehead. "Are you okay, honey? You seem a bit pale."

No, Mom, I'm busy coming down from an almost panic attack. "Fine, Mom."

She sighs. "Okay, well, you can head home if you want. Your dad and I can finish up here. Get some rest."

Liam returns minus the nosy Nelly. "I can walk her home."

I turn to him, embarrassed. "You don't have to. You live right here in town. It's out of your way."

"No trouble." Grabbing my jacket, he hands it to me, then says bye to my parents and escorts me out of the store.

Quiet falls between us, with the birds and squirrels wrestling in the trees as background noise. It's not until we're halfway home that I break the silence.

"Tell me something I don't know about you?" Liam looks down at me, and I stare straight ahead, suddenly feeling silly for the question. "Stupid thing to ask, don't—"

"I'm allergic to sumac."

I look back, giving him a side-eye.

"I'm serious," he says. "When I first got over there, they stationed me in a small town, handing out meals and school supplies to kids. This mom…she was so grateful for the supplies, she insisted on making me some food for my journey home. I said yes and sat down while she made this pita sandwich. Anyway, I ate it, thanked her, and went on my way. A few minutes later, my throat started feeling really scratchy. Shortly after that, I was struggling to breathe. I made it back to camp before I dropped dead. Thankfully there was a volunteer in the medical field, and he stabbed me in the leg with an epi-pen. At first, I thought she poisoned me. But the side effects I was having pointed to an allergic reaction. It wasn't till later when I did a full blood panel and realized it was due to a spice she used. Sumac."

I stare at him, bewildered. I wish I could claw into his brain and learn all his secrets. His journeys. What it was like to be over there. Was he ever scared? Was he ever in danger?

"Okay, enough about me. Your turn. What happened back there?"

I shrug, staring forward. "I just don't want to talk about it. Is that okay?" Because I can't. Because hiding behind a lie seems easier. I pick up my pace, needing to get home. Be alone. Work on the demons battling in my head. I want to be honest, but with that comes judgment. Scrutiny. I go from being this perfect daughter to the family train—

"Ouch!" I yelp as something cold smashes against the back of my head. I turn around to Liam, holding a snowball.

"What the! Oh, don't you—"

I duck, missing the next one. "You're gonna get it." He takes off down the sidewalk. Grabbing for a pile of snow, I chase after him. "Come back here!"

"No, I'm good." He hides behind the tree in front of my house.

"Oh, like I can't see you. I see some things never change."

"And what's that?" he asks, peeking his head out, dodging the flying snowball.

"That you suck at this game." I pick up more snow.

Another perfect ball. The closer I get, the more my adrenaline spikes. I might have ammo, but he has strength and height. "Come out, come out, and get what's coming to—" I squeal as he rushes at me. I don't even have time to cock my arm back before he picks me up and throws me into a pile of snow.

A vibrant array of curse words sits at the tip of my tongue. Dropping to the ground above me, he presses his lips to mine, and everything fades as I sigh into his kiss. It's gentle and sweet, sending a warm tickle down to my toes. He pulls away, and my eyes flutter open to the most enchanting sight. "Holly Bergner, will you go to the Winter Wonderland Festival with me?"

"Why, Liam Cody, are you asking me out?"

"That I am. Friendship date, of course. Unless you say no. Then I'll be forced to ask old Mrs. Power—*ouch*."

I pinch his thigh. "Shut it. It's your lucky day. My schedule is pretty clear. So, yes. I will."

His smile is infectious. My mental camera clicks over and over, wanting to hold on to that smile forever. "Good." He drops his mouth to mine once again and pulls away, holding my gaze. "Well, I should probably let you up before your parents come home and catch me trying to seduce their daughter in the snow."

"It wouldn't be the first time," I say. "If I remember correctly, you couldn't keep your hands off me." Now I'm just playing with fire. There's a flicker in his eyes. One I remember well. It creates a slow burn inside me, melting the snow beneath me.

He stifles a grin. "Is that how you remember it?"

I shrug. "Sounds familiar. From. . .what I remember. . ."

He shakes his head, his smile touching my soul. "Whatever you say, Bergner. Pick you up at seven. Don't be late."

Chapter
eight

No. No. No.

I toss another shirt over my shoulder. Why did I not bring anything cute to wear! I tear off the turtleneck and dig back into my pile of failed outfits. Something in here has to say date outfit. Not that it's a date. *He did technically ask you out.* But did he *mean* a date? I haven't been on a date since... well, forever. Gah! "What does one wear on a freakin' date nowadays?"

"Honey, who are you talking to?"

I turn to my closed door. "No one, Mom. Sorry!"

Okay. Pull it together. Keep it simple. Leggings. Off-the-shoulder sweater. Easy to take off—no! Full sweater. Jeans. Show no skin. This is not a hookup. We're friends. Going out and having a nice time. That hopefully leads to more hot sex—

"Shit!"

Sex just makes things complicated. Not that it isn't already. We're the walking definition of complicated. A tangled mess of what the hell are we doing. Torturing each other, for one. This won't end well for either of us. Even the sirens are going off in my head. Abort. Abort. No, like, seriously. . .

I look around and dig under a pile of discarded clothes, finding my phone ringing. No sirens. Phew. I'm not completely crazy. Eileen's goofy face fills my screen.

"Hey, you."

"She's alive!"

I hold my phone between my ear and shoulder while I shimmy into a pair of jeans. "Barely. Hey, what does someone wear on a non-date date?"

"Uh, since when are you dating?"

"I'm not. Well… not really." I pair my jeans with a fluffy white sweater.

"Yeah, you're going to have to elaborate on that. You left here looking like a kid who lost her favorite stuffed animal and wearing a powdered donut mustache." Ugh… probably why these jeans are so tight. "Wait… don't tell me you ran into the one who got away."

More like collied with and slipped, spreading my legs. "Something like that."

"No *way*. Tell me everything!"

I stand in front of my mirror, twisting and turning. It's not my best, but it's not my worst. It'll have to do. Sighing into the phone, I say, "I don't even know where to start. I told myself I wouldn't search him out. If I ran into him, so be it. That door was closed, and there was no way I was opening it. Then that door opened, literally, and things have been insane ever since." I tug at my sweater. Maybe I *should* go with the off-the-shoulder—

"Girl, you sound love-struck."

"Ew, I do not!"

"Yeah, you do. You've sighed more times on this call than I've ever heard."

Great, not only am I love-struck, I'm turning into my sighing mother. "It's complicated. He's… this force of nature, and I'm a poor, helpless little leaf who doesn't stand a chance of not getting swept away. He's different and the same. And, well, he's really hot and great in bed, and I'm just digging myself a hole because I don't know what I'm doing!" She's silent for a beat, and I check to see if our call got disconnected. "You still there?"

"Yeah, sorry. Just had to grab my laptop. How do you spell this guy's name? You sold me on hot and sex."

"Just look up the definition of smoldering."

"What?"

Ugh. I'm losing it. "Nothing. Listen, I'm sorry to cut this short, but I have a thing." A non-date date.

Eileen laughs. "No problem. But speaking of *things*, Vincent has been by looking for you. Obviously, I didn't tell him where you were, but he was pretty insistent on wanting to see you."

Mood killer. "Tell him I died and to go get—" The doorbell rings, and I look at the time. "Shit, I've gotta go. I'll be home soon enough. We'll finish this talk."

"Don't rush home on my account. Maybe you should stay a little longer. See where things go with the hot-sex ex."

"Like I said, that ship has sailed. See you in a few days." I hang up, check myself one last time, and head downstairs for my non-date date.

When I make it to the bottom step, my eyes gravitate toward the doorway, and I inhale a sharp breath. Liam has always been handsome. From the depth of his eyes to the gentle curve of his lips, he wasn't just beautiful, he was intoxicating.

"There you are, honey," Mom says popping out from the kitchen. Liam breaks from the conversation he's having with my dad and looks up. Our eyes collide. The way he soaks me in ignites a tornado of butterflies inside me. "Oh wow, doesn't she look lovely, Henry?"

"She sure does," Liam responds instead. His eyes never waver from mine. Everyone else in the room suddenly fades away.

It scares me how he still has this power over me. My skin buzzes as my body comes alive. It's exciting yet frightening. We were going to be one of the greatest love stories. Then our story just ended.

I look away and inhale slowly. There's a sudden heaviness inside me, making it hard to breathe. So many buried emotions are surfacing, and I'm not sure how to decipher them. I want to wrap myself up in his arms and play out the next chapter in our story, but reality rears its head, ruining those childish ideas. I go back home soon. What happens to us then?

"Why the frown?" Liam asks softly as I make my way to him. Not realizing I have my emotions on full display, I shove my pending panic back down and muster up a playful smile.

Mom chimes in, saving me. "It's nice to see you two together again." *Not* what I expected her to say. My face turns the color of my maroon panties.

"Oh, we're not—"

"Like old times," Dad puts his unneeded two cents in.

"This isn't—"

"Remember that one year it snowed so bad, we worried they were going to cancel the festival. . ."

"Okay! We're leaving now. On our friendly walk to town." I grab Liam and drag him toward the door.

"You two have fun," Mom says, winking at me. I roll my eyes and pull a chuckling Liam out the door.

"I think she thinks we're on a date," Liam says, trying to keep up with me as I speed walk down the sidewalk.

"Well, she's wrong. This is just two friends."

"Two friends," he repeats, humor in his tone.

I slap him across the chest. "Stop. I mean it. The second those two get the wrong idea, my mom will pull out her wedding binder and start the planning."

"She still has that thing?"

I look at him. "You kidding me? She's never lost hope."

A group of kids jump out of the bushes, throwing snowballs at each other, then run off just as fast as they appeared. I turn to Liam. "Don't even think about it."

His mouth twitches. "Didn't even cross my mind."

"Lies," I scoff, bringing my eyes forward. "Your lips always twitch when you're lying."

We walk the rest of the way to town in silence. Every so often, his hand brushes against mine. I pretend not to notice, but there's no doubt my blushing cheeks give me away. Every house we pass is lit to the hilt with holiday lights and creative manger displays.

The first time my parents ever caught us in a compromising position was in our own manger display. My mom made me go to church the next day and apologize to God for disgracing the Lord's house, then sat me down for a very long talk about the birds and the bees.

"Are you thinking about when your parents—"

"Of course not."

Thank God we hit the edge of town. Turning the corner, the town square comes into view, full of bustling townspeople enjoying the festivities. The gigantic tree lights up the night sky. It sparkles brightly, tinsel glittering alongside the enormous ornaments and ribbons. I wave at Helen Grant, our next-door neighbor, and watch as her small children run across the street, holding miniature nutcrackers.

"Are we hitting up Mr. Garrison's hot chocolate stand first or the funnel cakes?"

My stomach growls. "Definitely funnel cake. I need a solid base before my stiff hot chocolate."

"You've got it." He catches me off guard when he grabs my hand and pulls me toward Kinsley's Candy

Shoppe. A giggle falls from my lips as we zigzag through the crowd, Liam making comments like, "Sorry, we have a starved sugar freak. She bites when she hasn't had sugar. Excuse us, manic sugar patient."

"Hey, Mrs. Kinsley." He stops at the food cart outside the candy shop.

"Liam Cody. I heard you were back. Been hearing all the good you've been doin'. Your father would've been proud."

Liam's smile falters a smidge at the mention of his dad. I remember getting a call from Dad telling me about the heart attack and how his father didn't make it.

"That's very kind of you to say."

"And look at you two. Welcome home, Holly. Your mother has been telling the entire town how you finally made it home for the holidays. Funny to see you two together. You were always attached at the hip. Are you— did I miss something?"

"Oh, no, no. We're just fri—"

"Just hoping we can get one of your finest funnel cakes," Liam intervenes. Mrs. Kinsley's face lights up, and she nods, grabbing a fresh plate and sprinkling on a heavy amount of powdered sugar. I can't help it. I lick my lips. Liam chuckles as he reaches out and accepts the plate. "Looks amazing, as always. How much do we owe ya?"

"On the house. Thanks for your service."

"Thanks again." Liam nods and steps away while I try to snatch the plate out of his hand. He knows my end game and pulls it back before I make contact. "Easy there, killer."

"Give it to me."

"Or what?"

"Or I may just bite your hand off. You know it tastes

the best when it's fresh. The powdered sugar is still fluffy and melts in your mouth."

His eyebrows hike up. "Are we still talking about funnel cake?"

*Oh, that little. . .*I slap his chest. "Yes. Now give me a bite."

"Say please."

"Liam," I warn. He pretends to almost drop it, and I squeal. "Liam, seriously. Give me a bite. And if you drop it, I will most definitely just eat it off the ground. Nothing this delicious should go to waste."

Liam throws his head back and laughs. "I admire your dedication, Holls." He rips off a piece of cake. "Open up."

My hands go to my hips as I eye him. "Seriously?"

"How much do you want the bite?" He starts to lift the piece to his mouth, and I swat at his arm.

"Okay! Fine." I open my mouth, anticipating the moment the warm dough hits my lips. He takes his time lifting his fingers to my mouth. The damn smirk creeping along his face is going to get him a sock in the junk.

"Not gonna lie. I like you like this." I'm suddenly frozen, my jaw suspended while his words sink in. His eyes light up, and he gently strokes the warm dough against my bottom lip. I hold my breath, unsure what I want more, the sugary bite or the taste of his sultry lips on mine. So much so, I wet my own lips and shiver at the thin brush of sugar, anticipating both. I lean in, ready to—

"Liam? Liam Cody, oh my god!" We both turn to the woman inching her way between us. "I knew it was you. Mary. Mary McCallister. We went to high school together."

Liam drops his arm, along with my bite, and forces a smile. "Hey, yeah. How's it going?"

"Just enjoying the night. Wow, you look great." She

raises her dainty hand and brushes it up and down his arm. "My goodness. So strong." My lips purse at the way she squeezes his bicep.

"Thanks. Do you remember—"

"Oh, no, thank *you*. Heard you were away serving our country. Thank you for your service." She sways her hips, showing off boobs she certainly didn't have in high school. Liam doesn't seem bothered by her hands on him, and it irritates me. She moves in closer, sniffing the funnel cake —*my* funnel cake. "Oh my lord above, that smells heavenly. Think you can spare a bite?" Then she opens her mouth.

My jaw drops in absolute shock. Is this chick for real? Even worse, Liam just stands there! If he even dares. . .

His eyes drop to the funnel cake then back to her.

Is he—is he *considering* it? My hands form into tight fists. Clenching my jaw, I clear my throat loudly, which may come out more like a growl.

Finally, she turns to me. "Oh, hello."

"Oh, yeah, *hey*."

"You look familiar. Do we know each other?"

That's it. I'm ripping out her weave. I take a step toward her—

"Mary, this is Holly."

Mary looks as if she's struggling with her last brain cell to figure out who I am. "Oh, Hillary, right? I think I remember you. Wait…weren't you two, like, an item for a little bit in high school?"

I sneer at her comment. "Weren't you, like, voted Willow Falls' biggest slu—"

"Okay! Holly and I were going to check out the ginger-bread house station. Hear it's a real doozy this year. Nice seein' you." Her red lips part, wanting to say more, but Liam rips his arm from her grip, reaches for my hand, and walks us away.

"Can you believe that chick? Hillary. Like she didn't remember my name when you just said it. And an item for a little bit. *Seriously*? We were inseparable. Practically attached at the hip. We didn't even look at anyone else the whole time we dated!" Liam just stares at me. "Are you going to say something?"

"Are you jealous, Holls?"

I scoff. "Oh, please. Why would I be jealous? We're just frien—"

Liam cuts me off and drags me away from the crowd and into the alley, pressing my back up against the brick wall. "And how's being just friends workin' out for you?"

His mouth crashes against mine, passion igniting between us. His tongue parts my lips, my composure evaporates, and I forget we're in a place where anyone could catch us. I kiss him back, my own desire revving up. I wrap my arms around him, needing more. The funnel cake hits the ground as he seizes my hips and presses me up against the brick building. The sound of his deep moan, the sweetest melody, excites me, and I spin out of control. Everything about him is fueling my need, and I can't even remember what had me so worked up in the first place. The only thing on my mind is his lips on mine and how I never want them to be elsewhere. Well, maybe a few other places.

All too soon, he slows down, and reluctantly, I allow him to pull away. "You better?"

"Hmmm… I think so." As long as not feeling my legs isn't a concern.

"We still just friends?"

"The best kind," I sigh. I blink away the fog, my eyes fluttering open to the most beautiful sight. His eyes searing into mine. His lips are swollen, ravaged, aching for more. Embarrassment creeps along my cheeks at the way I acted.

The jealousy that burned inside me. He wasn't hers to touch. He's mine. He watches me. Knows the thoughts running through my mind. When my frown returns, I say, "She was going to eat my funnel cake. That was just a no-no."

Liam's cheeks dimple as he fights back a laugh. "It sure is." He leans in for another earth-shattering kiss. Mayor Riley's voice carries through the loudspeaker, and he stops. "We should get back out there."

We should stay in this little nook forever. "Yeah," I reply, and he slowly releases me.

He holds his hand out. "After you."

"Yep." I brush my hands down my jacket to gather myself, then turn on my heel and walk away, not stopping as I cock my head back. "You owe me a funnel cake." His laughter causes my heart to skip a beat, and I swallow down the emotions he creates inside me.

We reenter the bustling crowd of townspeople. Everyone has gathered around the stage, and the mayor and his wife are handing out candy canes to children. "Hello, Willow Falls," he begins. Liam stands next to me, close enough that our shoulders brush. "We're thrilled to see so many of you here tonight. What a special holiday. In just a moment, Willow Fall's finest elementary students will be performing this year's Nutcracker. But before we get started, I hate to mention this, but Mr. Fairchild fell this morning and broke his hip. He'll be all right, but he won't be able to lead the veterans' float. So, we were hoping…" He looks into the crowd, "our very own hero, Liam Cody… You've done such amazing things for our country. And we would be thrilled if you rode on the veterans' float in the Christmas Eve parade."

Approval and clapping echo in the square. Liam raises

his hand, thanking everyone, and nods. "I'd be honored. Thank you."

"No, thank you. Now, I think these little dancers are ready to put on a show if everyone would direct their attention to the left stage."

The crowd migrates over to the performance. People shake Liam's hand and thank him as they pass. My heart feels like it's going to burst with pride. I may not have been there to support him through this journey, but I'm still so proud of what he's accomplished. He's an honorable, selfless man.

I wrap my arm around his, tugging him close while we walk over to the stage. "What's this about?"

"Nothing. Just proud of you. I'm glad to call you my friend."

He releases a soft, partly suppressed laugh. "The friend thing. Got it. Let's go watch some sugar plum fairies and get you that funnel cake, *friend*."

I offer him a cheeky smile. "You had me at funnel cake."

We spend the rest of the evening in our own little bubble, watching the performance and listening to the carolers. We walk from booth to booth, admiring all the holiday crafts and even partake in the gingerbread house contest. By the time the night ends, I've fallen down this rabbit hole of the old Liam and Holly. As if time and regret don't stand between us. He offers to walk me home, and I tell him I'd rather walk him home.

The second we're through the threshold of his apartment, I'm in his arms, and our lips fuse together. He lifts me up and walks us back to his bedroom. We fall onto his bed, our mouths never parting as we tear at each other's clothes. Our jackets are off. Liam tugs at my jeans while I push up his thermal shirt. He shoves my jeans down my legs, but they get stuck.

"Boots," he says. I wrestle them off, flinging one and knocking over a light. My sweater is over my head and tossed away, my bra goes bye-bye, and his mouth covers my breast, feasting on my nipple.

I moan, trying to get to his zipper. I'm so turned on, I can't stop shaking enough to get a good grip. "Your pants. Now," I practically growl. Holding himself up with one arm, he kicks off his boots and thrusts down his jeans and boxers. I wrap my legs around him, my pussy slick with desire. He's thick and hard against me. "Fuck. Condom." He reaches over to his nightstand, but I grab his hair and pull him back.

"I'm on the pill. Unless there's something I should know, if you stall another second, I'm going to—"

With one thrust, he powers into me. It's like Christmas coming early. A multitude of lights blast behind my lids, and I let out a long, breathless moan. He works himself in and out while his mouth does magical things to my breasts. My entire body is on fire. My heart is beating like a freight train. I need more. So much more. My fingers thread into his hair, and I pull him toward me, needing his mouth back on mine. He kisses me with a ferocity that almost blinds me. His rhythm increases, and I pull in a tight breath, bucking my hips to meet his every thrust.

"Liam," I whimper, riding his cock.

He gathers my hair into his fist and slams his mouth back over mine. Feral and demanding. A silent message. *You were mine once; you'll be mine again.* He plunges into me over and over, grabbing the back of my thigh to extend my leg, allowing him to thrust deeper. My words become trapped in my throat. Wanting to beg for more. Tell him I belong to him. That he branded my soul a lifetime ago, and that has never faded. My orgasm builds, and small mews of pleasure fall off my tongue.

It becomes too much, and I break. Every nerve-ending in my body detonates as my sex violently spasms. I arch my head back and cry out from the most earth-shattering climax. Liam rides me hard and fast, growling out through his own release.

Liam's arm gives out, and he collapses against me. I can't catch my breath. My toes are tingling. My sex is still pulsating. "Shit," I choke out, not sure I'll ever fully regain feeling in my legs. Liam lifts, suppressing a smile. "Well shit. At least *you* don't have to put a shirt back on. We never took that bad boy off."

Fighting that devilish grin of his, Liam bends down and places his lips over mine. The only soft thing about him. Because he is all man. "Didn't think you could see it since you knocked out the light with your boot-kicking kung fu."

Oops. "Yeah, sorry about that. Desperate times. But I would suggest next time we remove the shirt. The whole eight pack and pure steel thing is kind of a turn-on."

"So, there's gonna be a next time?"

"A few times. Unless you can't—you don't think he—"

"Oh, he will."

Like a kid in a candy store, I match his playful gaze and spank his tight tush. "I gotta get up real quick. Text my mom that I'm sleeping at a friend's again so she doesn't worry."

He snatches me back, the hard feel of him against my stomach telling me I don't have time because he's more than ready to go.

"That's gonna have to wait 'til our next intermission. I've got to prove my stamina."

Chapter nine

The sound of Liam's alarm wakes me. I stir, shoving my face farther into his soft pillow, enjoying his warm body nestled up behind me. It's heavenly waking up like this. Now, if only his alarm clock would shut up.

"Liam," I mumble. "Turn your alarm off."

"That's not my alarm. I think it's your phone."

My phone?

"Oh shit!" I pop up. "I never called my mom last night." She probably thinks I'm dead in a ditch somewhere. I scramble out from under my warm cocoon and dive to the floor in search of my jeans. The ringing stops. Then goes off again. "Her wrath is on you." Where are my jeans?

"My fault?"

"Yeah! You held me captive. Don't deny it." My phone stops ringing. A few seconds pass, and it wakes up again. "Where is that damn—"

Liam sits up and helps in my search. My poor mother. He pulls up my jacket and reaches into my pocket, pulling out the phone. He looks at the screen, his easy-going smile faltering.

Shit.

Why do I have a feeling it's not my mother calling?

"Seems Vincent really wants to get in touch with you."

I jump up and swipe my phone from his hands. Not bothering to confirm who it is, I ignore the call. Eager bastard, because he calls right back.

"Wanna explain what that was all about?"

"Spam callers. You hungry? I still make a mean omelet—"

"Who's Vincent?"

Why do we have to go there? Everything is going so well. We're reconnecting and wrapped up in our perfect little bubble, pretending there aren't any outside monsters waiting to burst it. "My insurance guy?"

He doesn't join in my humor and abruptly stands, shoving himself into a pair of jeans.

"It's no big deal."

"No big deal." He throws on a Henley. "You know what? I've been trying to play this game. I really have. But I can't do it anymore."

"Do what? What game?"

"Really? Are we ever going to talk about it, Holls? The big fucking elephant in the room?" He swipes his hands through his hair. "You know, the fucking boyfriend you've failed to mention? The one blowing up your phone?"

"There's really nothing to mention—"

"You kidding me? How about that you fucking have one, and you've been sleeping in my bed?"

"Well, we don't really do much sleeping—"

"That's not the fucking point!" He digs his thumbs into his temples and clenches his eyes closed. His chest heaves as he takes in a deep breath then reopens them. "I've tried to give you time to tell me. Do you have any idea how hard it's been for me? Knowing I'm sleeping with someone who doesn't belong to me? You know how fucking *shitty* that makes me feel? But then I can't seem to stay away from you. Because I'm so goddamn in love with you still, I ignore everything else." He pauses, swallowing. His eyes are pleading as he continues. "Anytime anyone brings up something about your life, you shut down. Why? Is this all just an escape from reality for you? Playing house with me and getting me to fall for you all over again, just for you to leave? Who is he? Are you two serious? Do you *love* him?"

Guilt swarms in my chest as his confession tears at my heart. This whole time, while I've been avoiding being honest, he's been battling with right and wrong. He has every right to be mad. To even hate me. I wet my dry lips, my heart starting to race. "It's not what you think—"

He throws his hands up. "Jesus Christ, Holly, stop fucking hiding."

"I'm not!" My phone goes off again. I shut it off.

"Don't ignore it on my account." He turns his back on me and disappears into the bathroom.

"Liam, please. It's not what you think." I find my jeans and hurry into them, along with one of Liam's discarded shirts. "I'm not hiding anything. It's just…"

He returns. "Answer me this, what are we?"

"I don't understand."

"What. Are. We? What are we doing here?"

I open my mouth, but nothing comes out. There are so many things I want to say. Confess. But I'm frozen in this dimension of freaking out and really nervous. So, I say nothing. My silence gives Liam the wrong idea, and he exhales in defeat.

"Nice, Holls. Real fucking nice." Shoving past me, he walks to the front door and slides into his boots.

"Where are you going?"

"I need some space."

"From what? We're in the middle of a conversation."

He turns, his sullen eyes devoid of hope. He shakes his head. "No. I was in the middle of hoping, even though I've gone along with this whole friendship game, that our feelings were mutual. I guess I was wrong. I read us all wrong."

He turns again and opens the door. Panic seizes my lungs. The thought of confessing my awful truth scares me, but him walking out of my life again scares me even more. He has one foot out the door when I finally speak.

"Because none of it is true."

He stops and slowly turns to me. "Us?" I suck in a sharp breath as a knife slices into my chest. How could he ever think the last few days between us have been fake? "Gee, thanks for clearing that up—"

"My life. My job. The boyfriend," I scoff. "My perfect life. I lost my job a month ago. My mom is so proud of me, and I didn't have the heart to tell her. So... I've been lying to her."

"Why would you lie about something like that? You know your mom wouldn't judge you."

"But she would've felt sorry for me. And I don't need anybody pitying me."

He hesitates before he asks the next question. "The boyfriend?"

"Same as the job. Gone. I underestimated my worth." I laugh cynically. "He cheated on me." I break eye contact. "I lied. I was just ashamed. I got cheated on. Who wants to admit that? I came home to get away from it. I never planned on staying long. Certainly never planned on you being here. But here you are." I swallow, forcing down the lump in my throat. "And before I knew it, I got caught up in this little game of 'let's pretend my real life doesn't exist while our old perfect life never stopped.'"

He continues to stare at me but doesn't attempt to ease any of my guilt. His lips draw together. The only movement is the ticking of his jaw. "Are you going to say something? Tell me to leave? Call me a liar? Shit, call me whatever, just say something." Tears pool in my eyes. I know I fucked up. His pinched lips and hard expression tell me so. A tear cascades down my cheek, and I take a deep breath to rein in my emotions "Okay then. Well…I guess the silent treatment should tell me enough."

He releases the door, taking a few steps toward me. My heart beats out of my chest. I'm practically choking on my guilt. Maybe this is where he throws me out. "Listen, no need to drag me out of here. I'll leave on my own. Again, I'm really. . ."

My words die off as the tips of his boots touch my bare feet. He reaches out, cupping my neck. "Look at me." I dread seeing the disappointment in his eyes. I lift my lashes to meet his. "You shouldn't lie to your mother. She loves you no matter what. And losing your job or having some piece of shit guy who doesn't know what he has won't change that for her."

We stare at one another, his thumb caressing the back of my neck, creating a wave of heat.

"And Vincent? Are you done with him?"

"So done. Like done and more done."

More silence falls between us. I feel like I'm going to combust.

"Don't lie to me. Don't ever fucking lie to me again, Holls."

I nod like a goddamn bobblehead. "I'm not. I won't." I squeal as he picks me up over his shoulder, startling me. "Oh boy. Does this mean you're not mad at me?"

"It means I'm mad as hell you lied to me." Another squeal rips from my throat when he spanks my ass. I'm tossed onto the bed, and in a blink, he rips my jeans down my legs.

"Is this, like, my punishment? Because I've probably

lied about a few other things," I pant, anticipating what's coming.

"Oh, this is your punishment, all right. When you're begging for me to let you come, you really will be sorry." His mouth drops to my sex, and a deep moan falls off my tongue.

My fists grip the sheets as he laps at me, attaching his mouth into my slick heat. He's not gentle. More like ruthless and demanding. A man making his claim. His tongue plunges into me, and I buck my hips, riding his mouth.

"Oh, Liam. *Shit.*" That didn't last long. I grind into his mouth, my orgasm within reach. Then his mouth is gone. "What are you doing?" Oh, God, please don't let this be my—

"Grounding you." He climbs off the bed, forgetting we were just in the middle of something very, very important.

"I thought that's what you were doing? I've been bad, and you were going to punish me. With, like, your tongue."

His dark laugh tells me we're not on the same page.

"I'm teaching you a lesson. Now, I'm gonna run to the store and get the ingredients for that omelet you promised me. Don't even think about finishing."

I sit up. "Are you for real right now?" I am *not* opposed to humping the bed if he seriously leaves me like this.

"Dead serious. Do you still love ham?"

He has to be fucking kidding me right now. "You better be kidding. And yes, of course, I still love ham." How is he walking away from this right now? He looks like he's about to tear a hole in his jeans! Just like that, he turns around and walks out of his bedroom. Seconds later, the front door opens and closes.

❄

I forgo humping the bed. Instead, I pace around his apartment. I get it. He's mad I lied. I would be too. But to deny me. . .To put me in this kind of situation. *So* not cool. And how could he just stop? There was no way he's not turned on. The monster in his pants proved otherwise. If he thinks he's getting an omelet out of me before he finishes what he started, he is absolutely nuts. Maybe I should just leave. Show him who's boss. He's not going to bring me to the highest peak just to leave me hanging. And dammit, my nipples are still hard. I should take a shower. No, I should just leave! But I am kind of hungry. And my vagina is hungrier.

Jesus, did I just use the word vagina?

Is it getting hot in here?

I feel my forehead. Maybe I should sit down. Nope, maybe I should stand. Maybe I should—

The sound of the door unlocking triggers me. Liam isn't even through the threshold before I jump him. My lips are on his so fast, I don't care that he drops the bag. A low growl travels up his throat, and he kicks the door shut, slamming my back against it. I kiss him deep and hard, showing him who's boss, but it seems I'm dealing with a beast of a man just as starved.

He kisses me back, using a spare hand and shoves his pants to his knees. He rips my panties to the side and drives into me. We moan in unison. He pulls back, then plunges inside me over and over, every thrust hitting deeper. My entire body begins to vibrate. It's going to be mere seconds before I explode into a million pieces of pure ecstasy.

Liam hammers into me so hard, my lips part on a silent scream.

"Fuck, Holls," Liam growls, his own orgasm ripping through him, warmth filling me.

Taking a bite of my ham and cheese sandwich, I glance over at Liam, who's looking back at me with the most beautiful, easy-going smile. "How's your breakfast?" I ask.

"It's lacking the egg part of the omelet," he replies.

I take a bite of my food. "Well, that's your fault."

"My fault? You're the one who jumped me and made me drop the bag."

"Correct, but *you're* the one who left me high and dry—which *caused* me to jump on you and take what I rightfully deserved. And speaking of lacking—*owww*." I fake wince when he flicks my leg. "What's up with your tree? You normally go all out for the holidays." We glance at his pathetic excuse for a tree. "You have to admit, it's pretty sad looking."

Liam scratches his chin. "Dammit. It is, isn't it?"

I take another bite. With a full mouth, I reply, "Like, bad."

"Well, what do you say we fix that?" He doesn't wait for my answer. I'm up in his arms, waving bye to my discarded breakfast and the sad tree as he carries me down the hall.

"What do you have in mind?" I ask, eager to know his plans.

"For starters, I'm going to shower. With you. But I plan on making you very dirty before I clean you up. Then we're going out for a goddamn real Christmas tree."

My eyes light up. "Sounds like an eventful day. I need to check my schedule. Hmm. . ." I trail off when his lips touch mine. He cups my ass and kicks open the bathroom door, never pulling his mouth from mine. I love the way we mold together. The comfort of his touch. The familiarity of his body against mine. This was always us. Liam and Holly. Inseparable.

There's always been a powerful attraction between us. Years apart hasn't changed that. I wrap my arms around his neck and press my chest closer to his. The way his heart beats against mine, the pulse in his neck as he fights for control—every vital part of Liam Cody ignites this ache inside me. To make up for lost time. To confess I've never stopped loving him. Not even for a second.

I sigh, parting my lips. My body shivers as our tongues collide in a sensual dance. Leaning forward, he rests me on top of the vanity, then turns on the shower. He doesn't speak as he slowly removes my clothes, piece by piece. My mouth becomes dry at the sight of him as he starts to undress himself until each layer of clothing is removed. I gaze at my initials over his heart, stirring a flutter in my belly. My pulse races. I'm suddenly hyperaware of every part of his body.

Licking my lips, I say, "You know, on second thought, your tree is fine. There's really no need to leave your place today." Or ever… Liam chuckles, his lips curling into a cocky smile. He knows he's a god. "Or not. We should really get that tree—"

"Enough talking, Holls." He lifts me back up and steps into the steamy shower. I take a long breath as the hot water hits my back. He pushes me up against the tile, his erection resting at my sex. He stares down at me, peeling away every emotion stirring inside me. I rest my head against the tile, and he leans in, his teeth playfully grazing down my lobe. I sigh, opening my legs wider. He slowly grinds into me, and just the connection has me arching my back for more.

"We should probably hurry. Trees are flying off the shelves. Get this going." My sex pulsates with overwhelming desire. I'm about to start full-on threatening him if he doesn't—"Oh God," I moan as he slides inside me, my eyes falling shut. I press my lips against his and arch my breasts into his chest. The gentle stroke of his tongue is like heaven. I shiver as he pulls out and plunges back in. We're so close, so connected, that my mouth parts, so many confessions sitting on the tip of my tongue.

"Liam, Liam, Liam. . ." I say his name as I whimper and moan. My entire body tingles and my chest tightens. Tears fall from my eyes. I clutch Liam's shoulders as my orgasm rips through me.

"Fuck," Liam grunts, hitching my legs higher as he pumps into me, finding his own release.

I sag into the wall, hoping his arms don't give out. I can't feel my legs and will fall on my ass.

"Should I be worried that you're crying?"

"Nope. Just wires crossing. Pretty sure you moved some stuff in there."

He gazes down at me, watching. "For real. What? Do you want me to say it? Liam Cody, you're so amazing at sex that you make girls cry. Like *orgasmic* cry."

His chest rattles against mine. He shakes his head and runs his hands through my wet hair. "Then it's a good thing it's the holidays, and I'm in the giving spirit."

"What about this one?" I point to a huge fir tree.

"I know you want to compensate for my small tree, but that is about five feet taller than my ceiling."

I cock my head to the side and stare up at it. "I mean… maybe we just trim the trunk."

Liam grabs my hand and pulls me farther down the line. "What about this nice pine?"

"No. They shed needles."

"Holls, they all shed needles." We stop at a tree, both of us eying it. "Nice and thick. Looks sturdy."

I turn and ogle him. "We still talkin' about a tree, Cody?"

"Says the dirty bird who takes everything and turns it into something sexual—"

I slap him across his broad chest. "I do not."

"Oh, okay. So this tree. It's thick, just like you like it. And long, but apparently not as long as you prefer, hence the other tree. Oh, and would you say it's nice and wide too? Are you worried it's not gonna fit?"

Warmth spreads across my cheeks. I shake my head slightly as his relaxed smile grows into a full-blown grin. "Those flushed cheeks tell me you are not thinking about a Christmas tree."

I most certainly am not. "Shame there are such average trees here. It's been a while since I've truly seen a real girthy and full *tree*."

Liam throws his head back and bellows out a deep laugh. "You wound me, Bergner," he says, rubbing at his chest. I lift my chin, trying to mask my laughter. I steal a peek at him, and those damn butterflies go berserk again.

"Seriously, we need to pick a tree before the holiday is over."

Liam takes a deep breath and eyes the row of trees. "Okay. How about this one?" He takes my hand again and continues to walk us along. "A balsam fir. Gives us the perfect Christmas fragrance and is known for its sturdy branches. Perfect for decorating."

I stare at it, surveying the branches and perfectly round shape. Letting out a deep, gratifying sigh, I nod my head and give Liam a thumbs up. "I approve."

A cocky smile spreads across his handsome face. He

returns my nod and reaches in to grab the tree. Of course, I don't deny myself the eyeful of his tight tush.

The bell to the door rings as we enter the hardware store. I wave to Stew at the register, then weave in and out of customers toward the holiday section.

"They're busy today," Liam notes as we grab a cart.

"Yeah, it's all the people waiting 'til the day before Christmas Eve to put up trees." I wiggle my brows, reach for a set of lights, and toss them into the cart. "Soon, the humbug tree will be gone, and all will be right in the world." I look back at him, but he seems to have lost some of his playfulness. "Did you not want to get rid of it?" What did I say to change his mood?

Liam bends forward, grabbing a set of white ornaments. "Christmas hasn't been the same these last years. Just didn't feel right to keep up with all the good parts when the best parts were missing."

Shit.

Shit. Shit. *Shit.*

It's a hard pill to swallow, knowing I've been wrong this whole time. All this falls onto my shoulders and seeing Liam's beautiful smile dull guts me. I shift from foot to foot. Stuffing my hands into my pockets, I say, "Listen, Liam. I'm sorry—"

"There you two are." My mom's voice pulls me from my apology, and I slap on a cheeky smile.

"*Heeey*, Mom!" My voice cracks.

She takes us in as she approaches, then surveys our cart. "What are you kids up to?"

"Just getting lights and ornaments for Liam's tree. He

needed a new one. Bigger one. One that says he shouldn't dislike Christmas because of something—"

"What she's getting at is I needed a Christmas tree, and Holly helped me find one. We're just here grabbing some lights."

She shoots us suspicious glances. And then it happens. The sigh. The *you two are up to no good* sigh. "Okay then. Well, are you coming home tonight or having another sleepover? With Kelly Anne?"

My mouth opens and closes, but no words fall out. I clear my throat and break eye contact with my mom to look at Liam. "Well…ya know…it's been a long time. Just gonna do this tree and head back. So much to catch up on. We really missed—"

Liam saves me again. "I'll walk her down to Kelly Anne's when we're done."

What the hell is wrong with me? "So…we're just gonna get some stuff and be on our way. Love you." I lean in and give my mom a kiss on the cheek. She pats Liam on the shoulders then disappears with another damn sigh.

Not much more is said. A few *I like these*, and *what do you think of those?* It's not until we're back at his place with the tree wrapped in lights that I speak.

"She knows."

Liam hands me a glass of wine. "She doesn't."

"She totally knows. She gave me The Sigh. You know the one."

"And what exactly do you think she knows?" He takes a sip from his glass and sets it down. Opening a box of white ornaments, he hooks them, handing me one at a time.

"She knows we—we're up to something." I take the ornament and place it on a branch.

"And what is it we're up to?" He hands me another.

"Oh, come on, not catching up on local news and diets. We're, you know, doing it."

He bursts out a laugh and hands me an ornament. "Holls, we're not kids anymore. I'm pretty sure it's okay if your mom knows her adult daughter is having sex."

I take a hefty sip of wine. "Yeah, her daughter, who she thinks is in a serious relationship."

"You need to tell her the truth. I don't know how much longer I can go without kissing you in public."

That gets my attention. "You wanna kiss me in public?"

His lips curl into the most delicious smile. "I wanna do more, but yes. I want you on that float with me tomorrow. By my side. I want everyone to see how beautiful you are and be able to say you're mine." He hands me another ornament as if he didn't just unleash a panty-dropping confession. "Tell your mom. Ride the float with me tom—"

"I made a mistake," I spit out.

"You made a—"

"Don't speak! Just let me finish. I made a mistake. That night… I should have let you explain. If I had known everything, maybe things would have gone differently. I don't know if I would have gone with you or stayed. It hurt too much when Billy didn't return home. But you? I felt if I just separated myself from you, getting that call one day wouldn't hurt so bad. But being away hurt more. I would have nightmares that the call came and would wake up in hysterics. I was so fucking scared. You were asking me to be okay with you dying."

"I told you—"

"And I told you I would not have survived two deaths. I barely survived with my brother. You ripped my heart out the day you left, but I never tried to mend it. I never tried to call you or write to you. I knew what you were going to endure, but I was selfish and only thought about how I would feel."

He puts down the box of ornaments and grabs my wine, setting it on the table. "Holly, it's not like that."

"It is. And now, I just come storming back into your life, being all needy and obsessing over your thick tree and handsome smile and GI Joe persona." I throw my hands up in the air. "And I don't even know if you want me. Maybe this is all hate sex and you're just getting back at me for being a selfish human. I assume you still like me, but it would make sense...all the wild sex—"

"I don't know if I've ever just liked you, Holls. You've always been this constant part of my life. Whether you were here or not." He cups my face. "You don't owe me an explanation. I'm just as guilty. Let's be done pointing fingers and taking blame. We were young. We both had our reasons. Maybe this is how it was meant to be. Maybe we were always meant to find our way back to each other. Maybe *this* is our Christmas miracle."

I can barely see him through the tears. He's so selfless. Inside and out. That damn flutter fills me up, and I throw myself into his arms. He lifts me and carries me over to the couch. Taking a deep breath, I spill my heart out. "I never stopped loving you. I thought about you all the time. Even if I was with someone...nothing felt right. My heart never felt full because they were never you." His hand cups the back of my head, and he pulls me to him, his lips crushing against mine. "I love you. I've always loved you," I whimper against his mouth, refusing to let him go. His free hand grips my thigh, tugging me forward. Our bodies grind together, and a breathless moan leaves my lips. He slows down, and I draw back, worried.

"What? What's wrong?"

He brushes his thumb down my cheek as he stares at me with such a longing, touching every part of my soul. "I love you too, Holly Bergner. Fuck, so damn much." He takes my mouth in a savage kiss, parting my lips. His tongue claims mine, and we don't let go until I start to feel light-headed. He casually pulls back, catching my silly grin. He rests his forehead against mine. "What's so funny?" he asks, his hand brushing up and down my thigh.

"I still can't believe we're here. That you're here. That I'm in your lap." I laugh. "It just feels good. Like being home again. Really home."

"You are home." He takes my hand and presses it over his heart. "You're fucking home."

Chapter ten

I can't remember the last time I enjoyed Christmas Eve. The sound of carolers early in the morning. Liam's apartment smelling like fresh pine. The most wonderful man wrapped around me.

"Morning." Liam's hoarse voice hums in my ear as he tugs me closer. He kisses the back of my shoulder. "How'd you sleep?"

A small smile breaches my lips. "For the two hours we did, like a baby." When your man tells you you're his home, you have all-out, wild, maniac sex into the wee hours of the morning.

I roll over and stare into his sleepy gaze. "Hi."

"Hi." He tucks a strand of hair behind my ear, then presses a feather-soft kiss to my nose, then my lips. "I like you in my bed."

"Me too. I missed you. A lot. Just wanted you to know… if I haven't said it enough—"

His lips claim mine for a deeper, meaningful kiss. I hate that my emotions keep getting away from me. Everything about this moment is absolutely perfect, yet I wipe at tears on my cheek. Is this too good to be true? Am I dreaming? I press my lips tighter to his, and he flips me, digging his fingers into my hips.

"Why are you crying?" he asks, looking up at me. My

hands tremble as they glide up his bare chest, pausing at the ink over his heart.

"Tell me about your life out there?"

His body tenses, then just as quickly relaxes under me. His fingers caress up and down my thighs. "It was amazing, scary, thrilling, fulfilling, lonely. Being able to help someone unable to help themselves is a feeling I won't ever be able to explain, but there were a lot of struggles too. Leaders who didn't want us coming in and helping. Barriers we had to fight through daily. Once we completed the mission, I was going to come home, but I enlisted in the military. It was then that things got hard. I worked more in the field. Lots of rescue missions, which always seemed like suicide missions, but we suited up and did what we had to do. I met some great people, honest civilians who just wanted a better life. And some who wanted revenge because of a war that wasn't theirs to fight."

He stops for a moment then clears his throat. "But it's the job I signed up for. I had a great team. It still got lonely. I missed home. You. Didn't help that while I was away, my dad had a heart attack and passed."

My voice cracks with emotion. "I'm so sorry. I heard. I didn't know how to reach you, or if I could—"

"Don't be." My eyes blink rapidly, fighting back the tears as I bite down on my lower lip. He brushes his thumb along my lips. "We're here now. Together. Let's focus on that. It's all I care about."

With glistening eyes, I collapse against his chest and sweep my lips over his. "Deal." I kiss him as a vow, a promise, that this time, things will be different. He kisses me back, sealing it. Liam's alarm starts to beep, breaking us apart. He leans over, with me still smothering him, and shuts it off. "Liam, if the offer still stands, I would love to be with you on the float today."

His lips tilt into the most beautiful smile. "I'd love that."

"Yeah? Okay. Well, I need to do something beforehand. I need to go." I try to throw my leg off him, but he catches me, locking me in place.

"What do you have up your sleeve?"

I bend down and slap a quick kiss to his lips. "I need to make things right with my parents. Tell them the truth." Liam nods and releases me to get up. "No, you stay and get ready. I need to do this alone. I also need to shower and get clothes that aren't yours. I'll meet you at the square. Save me a spot?" I smile.

"Right next to me."

Another quick kiss, and I'm gathering my clothes and heading out. I skip the whole way home, practically shaking with excitement. The closer I get, the more that excitement turns into nervous jitters. By the time I'm opening my front door, I'm seriously debating aborting my mission.

"Mom? Dad?" I call out to a quiet house. The faint smell of coffee stirs in the air, but when I enter the kitchen, it's as clean as a whistle. "Hello? Anyone home?" I don't know whether to be disappointed or relieved. My heart starts to slow at not having to confess that I'm a lying, jobless, horrible daughter to my loving parents. But then, the float... How am I supposed to stand next to Liam, proudly, knowing my mom might judge me for my poor actions?

My parents always loved Liam. There was nothing harder than having to tell them we were done. They were so disappointed and hurt. And they didn't understand. Mainly because I never gave them a reason, then packed my bags to move to the city. Once my mom finds out we've reunited, she'll be over the moon. But they didn't raise a cheater. Infidelity is a no-no, and for me to be parading around town with my long-lost love while they still believe I'm still in a serious relationship is not okay.

I move into action, singing *'Tis the Season* throughout my whole shower, *Jingle Bell Rock* while I blow dry my hair and apply a light layer of makeup, and *I'll be Home for Christmas* while I dress in a cute pair of jeans and a fluffy sweater.

I'm humming *Silent Night* as I shuffle through my closet and reach for an old shoebox. Opening it, I grab the item on top.

"Give it to me!" I jump up and down in anticipation. I can't wait a second longer.

"No. What if you don't like it?"

"I'm sure I'm going to love it. Let me see it." I stick my hand out and tap my foot against the ground.

"It's just…you're so hard to shop for, and you wouldn't give me any ideas and kept saying you didn't want anything."

"I want you. That's all I need."

"Which makes it harder to find something for my beautiful girl when she has everything she wants."

I giggle, leaning forward and offering him a sweet peck on the cheek. "I do. Whatever it is, I'm sure I'll love it, so give it to me." I stick my hand out, and he places it on my palm. I clutch the little glittery box and pull at the green silk bow before lifting it open. My hands tremble. I'm speechless as I reach in and pick up the mistletoe. My eyes lift to Liam's as he fidgets.

"I know it's silly but—"

"It's not silly." My voice cracks.

"It's just…if all you want is me, I figured maybe I can just keep giving you parts of me."

"Can I see if it works?"

He nods, and I lift it above our heads. Our eyes lock, and I swear the lights on the tree sparkle a little brighter as he gives me the best Christmas kiss of all time.

I lift the artificial mistletoe to my nose, inhaling the faint potpourri-induced scent of pine and sweet berries. Liam never needed to shower me with material things to show his love. He just needed to give me him. And he did with every kiss. I can't fight the silly grin. I sigh happily. The chime from the grandfather clock dings, indicating I need to go. I jump into gear, hanging the mistletoe near the tree for when we return, and I won't have to hide how happy I truly am.

It's colder today, as I race down the street. My cheeks are a nice shade of red and I tighten my scarf. The town square comes into view and I look around for my parents. The entire town is in attendance. The tree glitters with the snow that fell overnight, and steam pours from the booths selling hot chocolate and homemade cider donuts. I wave at Mrs. Kinsley as I scan the crowd. Where are my parents? I need to find my mom. Everyone is starting to line up for the parade. Mayor Riley begins to address the town on the loudspeaker as I push through the crowd.

People shuffle closer to the curb. The parade begins, and the first two floats pass. I shift onto my tippytoes but still don't see Mom or Dad. "Shit," I mumble, unsure of what to do. Do I get on the float? Do I not? Ugh! I need to have faith that Mom and Dad will understand. I'll explain.

"I haven't missed him yet, have I?"

I turn to the voice next to me, finding Mary McCallister gazing over the crowd.

"Huh?"

"Liam. I haven't missed his float, have I? I really want to see him before he leaves."

What the fuck is she talking about? "Uh… no. And he's not going anywhere, not that it matters to you." God, once a snake, always a snake. I turn away, dismissing her, and do another scan. My phone vibrates in my pocket. Maybe it's Mom or Dad looking for me. I check it to see Vincent's name pop up. With a scowl, I click ignore and shove it back into my pocket.

"You don't know? Oh, but how would you? You're barely friends."

Okay. She wins. I turn back, giving her my full attention. "What are you yapping about, Mary? I seriously don't have time for your petty bullshit. Spit it out and be on your merry way." At least I still keep it holiday spirit-ish.

"Liam's deployment. They approached him the other day at the general store. Witnessed it myself. Such an honorable thing to head back into the trenches and fight for our country. You would think he's seen enough, but I guess there's nothing to see here, so there he goes."

A sudden heaviness slams against my chest. I shake my head in denial. Liam wouldn't do that to me. He wouldn't do that to us. "You're lying," I spit out, clenching my fists.

"Why would I lie?"

"Because you're a conniving bitch." She sucks in a breath while a few bystanders stare our way. Tears well in my eyes. I squeeze them shut to fight them back.

I inhale a staggered breath, then turn to the crowd as Liam's float comes into view. He's smiling. He looks happy. So damn happy. He signed up for another tour to leave me and didn't tell me while letting me fall back into this world of Liam and Holly.

Liam's float is in front of me, but I can't move. My feet are frozen in place, Mary's words still ringing in my ears. He stares at me, his smile slowly fading. Why would he do this? My hand shoots to my mouth, covering up the building sob. I sway on my feet and turn to push through the crowd when two hands grab me.

"Whoa, hey…"

My eyes shoot up at the familiar voice.

"*Vincent?*" I gasp. "What—what are you doing here?"

"I came to find you. You weren't answering my calls."

"For a damn good reason," I bite back. I realize he's holding me and push him away. "Let me go. We have nothing to talk about. You can leave." I try to push past him, but he jumps back into my peripheral.

"Please. Just give me a chance. I'm begging you."

My heart thumps wildly. I need to get out of here. I look over my shoulder at the float, where Liam stares at me intently, a fierce scowl across his face. I shake my head and turn back to Vincent. "Fine. Let's go." Without waiting to see if he follows, I move through the crowd until the warmth of the winter festivities is at my back. Each step I take, the coldness settles in.

"Thank you," Vincent says, trying to keep up with me. Every few seconds, he slips on a patch of ice, and I cross my fingers that he accidentally falls and breaks his neck. Sadly, we make it back to my house in one piece. I open the door and let it slam in his face. He takes the beating and walks in behind me.

I turn on my heel to face him. "You have thirty seconds."

He fumbles with his words. "I wanted to tell you how sorry I am."

"Great. Now, leave—"

"Wait! I really am. What I did. . .it was wrong. I wasn't thinking. I was working so much and tired, and Meredith saw the weakness in me."

If my eyes bulged any farther out of my head, they'd fall out. "Weakness? What exactly was your *weakness*, Vincent?"

"She tempted me. She knew how much I loved you, and she tempted me."

He's going to die now. *A Merry, Merry Murder* is going to be the title of my Lifetime special. A laugh rumbles out of me, then turns into a shrieking scream as I pull at my hair, needing this insanity to go away. "Your only weakness is you're a cheating piece of shit. You weren't tempted. You just didn't love me enough to be faithful to me. And that's your loss. Because I'm pretty fucking awesome!"

My face must match the color of the red bulbs hanging from our tree. I debate taking a swing at him but breathe past it. Violence is not the answer. "You know what? I don't care. We're still done. Please just leave."

Vincent takes a calculated step toward me. "Holly, please." He puts his hands up in surrender, acknowledging my bared teeth. "I want to make things right. You can have your job back. I spoke to Benjamin. He wants you back. Not only that, but he wants to promote you to Creative Director."

Okay, dammit, he's got my attention there. "What do you mean, promote me? He *fired* me."

"Yes, but I spoke to him and convinced him what an asset you are. I explained the whole meltdown at work was my fault. I fired Meredith. She's gone."

I ignore all the jibber-jabber about Meredith. That ship has completely sailed and sunk. But my job... I loved my job. I worked so hard to get where I was.

I glance at him, trying to figure out the catch. He takes a step toward me, and I back up, putting more distance between us. "What's the catch here?"

"No catch. Well, one...forgive me?"

And there it is. I refuse to be held captive or feel inferior to a man. Not anymore. I shake my head. "No." I move toward the door to kick his ass out, stumbling back a step, when he falls to his knee. My mouth hits the floor when his hand disappears into the pocket of his parka, and he pulls out a black box.

"Oh, no—"

"Holly, I made a mistake. I love you. We were good together. We can be again. This is what you wanted. So, I'm giving it to you."

"This is *not* how I wanted it. And I wanted it years ago." My voice shakes. I rub my hands down my face, unsure how this is happening to me. "Get up."

"Not until you say yes to me. You love me—"

"Get up—"

The front door opens, cutting me off as my parents walk in with Liam behind them.

"Honey, are you okay? Liam said you ran—oh dear. . ." My mom takes in Vincent, down on one knee, holding out a ring. Fuck. "Oh my goodness, did we just walk into? Are you two—"

"No," I spit out while "Yes" comes out of Vincent's. My mouth drops. I gaze down at him, murder in my eyes, and debate on kicking his teeth in. He sees the threat and quickly stands, turning to my mom.

"Hello, you must be Margaret. Your daughter has told me so much about you." My mom blushes and reaches out to shake his hand. "I just want to tell you I love your daughter immensely and hope you give us your blessing—"

"I didn't say—"

"Oh, um...of course. Henry, how wonderful is this?" She turns to my dad. He doesn't move a muscle. My gaze moves from my nervous looking mom to my frowning dad to a furious Liam. My mom catches wind, worry suddenly replacing her excitement. Her gaze flits around the room until it lands back on me. "Well, should we celebrate?" Rubbing her hands down her jacket, she continues. "I can put the roast in the oven early. I already have the pies—"

I step toward my mom. Vincent gets the wrong idea and steps in front of me. "Mom, no pies. No—"

Dad interjects. "Oh, honey, you put up the mistletoe. What a nice surprise. And look, you two lovebirds are under it." Dad points up to the mistletoe I hung. "Wait, isn't that the one you put up every year for..." His comment fades off as he looks between me and Liam.

I stare at Liam as he slowly brings his gaze from the mistletoe to me. My lungs constrict. I suck in a hard breath. His Adam's apple bobs as he swallows deeply, his eyes full of betrayal and the burning question: *How could I?* I open my mouth to explain, but he beats me to it.

"Well, it looks like she's doing just fine. Didn't mean to worry you both. I'm just going to head out." Then he turns to walk out.

"Liam, wait," I call out, but he doesn't stop. I rush past my parents. Vincent calls out to me, and I turn around, ready for battle. "You're crazy to think I would get back together with you. Insane. As for the job? Hard pass. I wouldn't give another ounce of my time to a company that undervalues its employees and clearly favors men over women. Especially if it was that easy to have your golfing buddy fire me to avoid your own name being smeared in the mud." I huff out an angered breath. "And it's a hell no on the proposal. Get out of my house before you meet my dad's shotgun." With that, I shift on my heel and race out the door after Liam.

"Liam!" I yell his name as I run after him. Damn, he's pretty fast. "Seriously, stop. That wasn't what it looked like."

He slams on his heel and turns around. I skid to a stop, almost sliding into him. "What do you want, Holls?

Congratulations? Sorry, I'm kind of out of those." He spins and treks faster down the street.

"Liam, stop!" When he doesn't, I throw out a low blow. "Running again?" He halts, slowly turning to face me. I suck in a deep breath at the tick in his jaw, instantly regretting my words. "I just wanted you to stop. I didn't mean it."

"Oh, you meant it. You've always said what's on your mind. You get caught and spew truths. You blame me, and I get it. But this?" He waves behind me. "This is low."

I flinch at his sudden coldness. "You have no idea what you're talking about. Back there, it wasn't—"

"So fucking sweet. Hope you two have a great life together." Once again, he dismisses me. I bend down and pick up a pile of snow, whipping it at his back. When he turns back, a pulsing vein protrudes out of his neck. Shit. "What more do you want from me? You want a reaction? Well, here it is. You're a liar. Spewing all this bullshit to me, sleeping in my bed, and for what? Just to go back to him?"

My mouth drops at his accusation. "What—no—you know what? While we're here calling each other out, why don't we talk about your deployment? When were you going to tell me about *that*?" He goes completely still. "Who's the liar now?"

"Say what?"

"Oh, okay. Hey, Holly, before I confess my everlasting love for you, let me tell you I'm being deployed again!" I scream.

"What the fuck are you talking about?"

"Don't play coy with me. Mary told me everything. She saw you with a recruiter the day you went out for eggs. Said you signed up for another tour. And to think spilling my heart to you might have actually meant something."

"Holly—"

"No! Don't you Holly me! I was committing to you. I meant it when I confessed my love for you. And I meant it when I said it was only you."

Liam throws his hands up. "Then what the fuck is that idiot doing here?"

"He just showed up! He begged me to talk, and it was right after Mary got to me. I said fine because I needed to get out of there. I was going to offer him thirty seconds and a kick in the ass on the way out, but then he started babbling, and before I could toss him to the curb, he was on one knee!"

He stares at me, his chest heaving. He rubs the back of his neck, and I wait for him to tell me off and turn around again. I won't be opposed to jumping on his back this time.

"Are you going home?" he asks, worry in his tone.

"I don't know," I reply with honesty. I love Willow Falls, but there's so much more to offer outside this small town.

"Do you plan on staying?" he asks again.

"I don't know that either." If he's leaving, there's no reason for me to stay.

He swipes his hand down his face, releasing a heavy sigh. His tone has lost its bite. This time when he speaks, it creates a knot in my belly. "Then what are we doing here? Why are we putting each other through this if we can't decide what we want?"

"I do know what I want. But I know I can't stay here while you leave me again. I won't lose you twice. For you to do so after everything we've gotten back makes me question what all of this has been." My voice sounds broken. Pained. My shoulders slump in defeat. I wipe at a chilled tear, fighting for a strong breath. "Maybe you're right. Maybe this was just us trying to relive a past that's just that."

Liam walks toward me, stopping when his boots touch

mine. He gently grabs my chin, forcing my tearful eyes to look at him. "Not a day went by that I didn't regret leaving you. I can't tell you how many times I wanted to quit and come home. Find you and tell you we belonged together. I was living half a life without you. And then, you were here, and my heart started beating again. This warmth melted the cold inside me. I didn't care about the past or the time we spent apart." His thumb brushes along my lower lip. "Because just seeing you brought me back to life. Nothing else in the world compares to you. Even before I had you in my arms, in my bed, I knew I would never again risk losing you. I would choose you."

We stare at one another, tears soaking my face. "Then why are you leaving again?"

He brushes away a tear. "Holly, there wasn't a recruiter here. The person Mary saw me talking to was Jensen Weller's son, my dad's best friend. He's in town for his grandmother's birthday. Not everyone who wears camo is enlisted. Jesus. She was just trying to get under your skin."

My eyes widen. "Wait, you didn't—you're not leaving?"

"No. I never was."

More tears well up in my eyes and pour out. I grit my teeth. "That bitch baited me, and I fell for it." I'm going to stomp back over to the festival and rip her fake hair out.

"Holly."

Then rip each cat nail off one by one.

"Holly."

Her fake eyelashes.

"Holly!"

"What?"

"I love you." Leaning in, he presses his lips to mine in the most breathtaking kiss. He parts my lips with his tongue, inviting himself to explore my mouth. All the tension bleeds from my body as I sigh into our kiss, wrapping my arms around him. He devours my mouth until it feels like I'm floating.

"I love you too. Only you. Always you."

He deepens our kiss, stirring the nest of butterflies. I debate on dragging him to the nearest Christmas manger display and ripping all his clothes off—

"Holly." Behind us, Vincent says my name, killing our magical moment. I send up a small prayer that Santa falls off the roof and takes him out. Liam tenses, and we pull apart. "Hey, man." He waves at Liam, and I slap my hand against Liam's chest to stop him from going after him. "Holly, you mind if we finish that conversation. Inside. Without him."

Liam doesn't let my dainty hand stop him from stalking forward. As he approaches, Vincent cowers in fear. "Don't hit me, man."

Liam stands like a giant in front of him, crossing his arms over his chest. "I'm not gonna hit you, but I am going to give you a piece of advice. Steer clear of my girl. *My* girl. I don't know whether to knock you out for being a cheating piece of shit or shake your hand for sending her back to me. What I do know is if I ever see your face again or hear you're trying to contact her, I'll bust your face in. You get me?"

Vincent's mouth drops. His lips flap like a gaping fish, but nothing comes out.

"I'm going to need a commitment here." Vincent tries to look over Liam's shoulder, begging for my attention, but Liam takes a step closer, blocking me. He clenches his fist, and Vincent quickly forfeits.

"Yes, yeah, sure. You got it, man. I'll stay away. Maybe if I can just have a quick word—okay! Also got it. I'll just be… leaving then." He backs away and almost stumbles as Liam steps with him.

I hide my laughter as Vincent runs off toward his car, tail tucked between his legs. When his car lights disappear into the distance, Liam turns around and stares back at me.

"I think that went well."

A grin spreads across my face. "I think it went perfectly. But you called me your girl. Does that stand? Am I really your girl?"

With a slow prowl, he moves into my personal space. I have to lift my head to keep eye contact. He stands before me like a soldier. My very own protector. Guardian of my heart and soul. He cups my face, caressing his thumb along my cheek. "You've always been my girl." His gaze unwavering, he pulls me into him, his lips a hairsbreadth from mine. "It's about time I show you just how much."

I bite my lower lip. "Hmm… what exactly do you have in mind?"

He brushes a strand of hair behind my ear. "For starters, I want to take you home and show you exactly how and why you belong to me. Relish in every delicate inch of your body so you know just how beautiful you are to me. What you do to me. And how I will spend the rest of my life cherishing you in every single way."

"Oh…?" It's all that comes out. My only thought is that the closest Nativity scene is in Mr. Johnson's front yard. "That sure is a selling point," I hum, gazing over his shoulder at the glowing hut. I clear my throat. "Sounds like you want to plant some roots."

His eyes fire up with passion. His intense gaze activates that flutter and my cheeks grow hot. He tugs me closer. "I'm going to be planting all right. First, planting my cock deep inside your sweet little pussy."

I shiver in his hold. "Oh boy."

"Then, together, we're going to build a plan. We're going to make promises. We're going to—"

"Okay!" I jump in his arms. He lifts me up as if I'm as light as a feather, and I wrap my legs around his waist. He instantly starts walking. "Where are you going?"

"We're going home to plant. Lots of planting."

I chuckle against his lips. "I think my parents are expecting us to come back. I did just make a scene and run out."

"Right." He digs for his phone in his jacket pocket. I raise a brow when he puts it to his ear. "Hello, Margaret… yes, I have your daughter. Yes, she's just fine. The roast sounds great, but first, I need to borrow your daughter for a bit."

I try to eavesdrop, but my mom talks so damn soft! He hangs up and shoves his phone back into his pocket. "What did she say?"

"She said how wonderful. She's glad to hear it."

"My mom said we were wonderful?" Such a mom thing to say.

"We are wonderful," he says.

"We sure are," I reply.

We make out like two teenagers all the way back to his place. By the time he's tossing me on his bed, I'm a goner. "This may be the best Christmas Eve ever," I hum against his mouth.

He sucks in my bottom lip then works his way down my neck. "Oh, baby, it hasn't even begun yet." Like a magic trick, all our clothes are gone, and he's driving home with me screaming, "Oh fu—"

✳

"Fa-la-la-la-la-la. . ." Christmas carolers sing next door while Liam and I stand outside my house.

"She's totally going to know."

"She's not gonna know."

"Mom is *totally* going to know. I'm pretty sure the flush in my cheeks is brighter than Rudolph's nose."

Liam looks down at me and chuckles. "You've always had that glow about you after good sex."

I slap him on the chest. "I'm being serious. I have to go in there and have a talk with my mom and explain to her why I lied, then stormed off, had amazing sex, and now we're back together, planting all sorts of roots." I wiggle my brows at the last part. Planting roots is my new favorite hobby.

"Don't look so stressed." He laughs. "It'll be fine."

"I'm not stressed. I'm happy. Ecstatic. My heart and my vagina are totally high-fiving." What did I just say?

"It's going to be fine, Holls." Liam opens the door, and the aroma of roasted lamb instantly fills my nose. I let out a long moan.

"Well, she's definitely going to know if you do that." Liam laughs.

"Oh, good, you're back. Dinner is almost ready. Holly, would you like to help me in the kitchen?"

This is it. The moment of truth. "Yep. I'd love to, Mom." I smile at Liam, leaving him to deal with my dad, and venture off into the kitchen. "Smells great," I say, walking in and picking up the lid off the gravy.

Mom sighs. "It sure does, doesn't it?"

Man, she wasted no time on the sigh. The *I know what you did* sigh. She pulls out the roast, and I stir the gravy. After stirring it to within an inch of its life, I spill my beans. "Mom, about what happened today. . ."

"Oh, honey, you don't have to explain to me."

"But I do."

She places the roasting pan on the stove and turns to me. Taking a deep breath, I close my eyes, and everything falls out. "Vincent and I aren't together. We haven't been for some time, which is a good thing since he's a cheating piece of sh...store bought pie." My eyes flash to her, then down again as I trail off. "Anyway, when I found out, I might have lost it on him and gotten fired in the process. I don't have all these perfect things. I should have told you, but I was embarrassed, and after losing Billy, I didn't want to disappoint you, and I'm in love with Liam, and we're going to plant roots. . ." Shit.

I stare at my mom, waiting for the judgement. Instead, her eyes glimmer with love. She leans forward, pressing her palm to my cheek. "Honey, I love you for you. You should never feel that you need to prove yourself as my daughter. You're the most beautiful soul, inside and out. Anything else that comes along is secondary."

Why is my mom so amazing? My throat grows thick with emotion. "I know that now. I just didn't want to disappoint you."

She strokes my cheek. "Holly, you will never disappoint me. You will always be my sweet, wild, beautiful, amazing child. You not having a job or a man who doesn't know how to treat you would never change that. Not to mention, I knew before you got here."

My eyes blast open. "Wait, *what?*"

Mom taps me gently on the cheek and bends down to check the roast. "Vincent called just before you got here looking for you. Chatty man he is. Babbles about as much as you do. And let me tell you, there were some things he could have kept to himself."

My jaw is dragging against the kitchen floor. "I'm not understanding—"

"I knew you two were broken up when you came home. I wasn't going to press you to tell me until you were ready. And then you looked a bit sidetracked..." She shuts the door and winks at me.

My eyes well with tears. She knew the whole time. "So then, the whole, *I'm also completely in love with Liam* part?"

She smiles back tenderly. "I already knew, honey."

"You did?"

"Of course I did. You would have to be blind not to see the way you two look at each other. Your father and I were like that when we were young. That crackle in the air when we were close. We couldn't keep our hands off each other—"

"Ew, Mom, I don't want to hear that."

"I'm just saying. I never believed that was the end of your story. Maybe you both needed to grow up. Become the people you needed to be before finding each other again. Not every road is paved in a perfect path."

Her words hold so much meaning for me. And maybe she's right. Sometimes love isn't a straight route. It's not always smooth. There are bumps and barriers, and sometimes people get hurt. In the end, Liam and I found our way home. And that will forever be our Christmas miracle.

I fall onto the bed, gasping for air, every muscle in my body limp. "Okay, *this* time, I think I'm seriously done." I rest my hand over my chest. "What's the average age for a heart attack? Am I too young to have one? I can probably have a heart attack, can't I? I think I'm having—"

"I think you're just spent." Liam breathes heavily, holding his own chest. "Damn, that was amazing."

I raise my head and stare down at my toes to see if they wiggle. "Shit. I think you paralyzed me."

Chuckling, Liam shifts onto his side and brushes a soft kiss across my forehead. "Maybe you shouldn't have teased me all throughout dinner."

"Teasing? I was hungry."

"Starving people don't seductively suck gravy off their fingers."

"My mom makes good gravy. I was savoring it."

"The pie?"

"I moan every time I eat her pie. It's delicious."

His face crinkles with laughter. "I see. So, you dropping whipped cream on your shirt then swirling it around with your finger?"

I suppress my own laugh. "I was cleaning it up."

"Yeah, yeah. I think you knew exactly what you were doing and got exactly what you intended."

That I did. A gratifying sigh escapes me. Life can be so unpredictable in the merriest of ways. Mom told me how happy she was for me. Dad was even happier. He'd always considered Liam a second son, and to have him become a permanent fixture in our life, I think it would help fill some of the empty space since Billy died.

We ate Mom's prized Christmas Eve roast and laughed and shared stories. Dad toasted to Christmas miracles, and Mom snuck little comments in about weddings and babies. My head was already spinning, and her questions made me even dizzier.

When Liam cut me off from the holiday wine, we said our goodbyes, and made it back to his place in record time, as he proceeded to show me how much I'm his in the most creative ways.

My cheeks burn at the giddiness forming in my chest.

"What are you smirking about?"

I roll onto my side to gaze at the most handsome person in all existence. "Just happy. Thankful. Not everyone has a mom who can cook a roast like—ahhh!" I squeal as Liam's fingers dig into my hips. "Okay, I'm kidding!"

"Can we be serious for a second?" His sated eyes become somber, and my smile falls. "Are we good?"

I stare at him, trying to decipher his question. "Yeah, why?" Does he not think we are? Shit. Am I reading this all wrong?

He strokes his fingers down the side of my cheek. "Because I want tomorrow to be the first Christmas of the rest of our lives. I want us to start fresh. Be done with the past, and let our mistakes stay there too. I don't want the guilt to hang over us, and to do that, we have to agree to let go. I know damn well I'll never make that mistake again with you, and I want you to know that."

I let out a huge breath. "I do too. I just want to be us. I mean, if you're in, I'm in." He leans in, his lips gently pressing against mine. A slight moan travels up my throat, and I part my lips, wanting more.

Liam grips my ass and tugs me forward, caging me against him. "Oh, I'm in, baby." And he seals the deal with the most devastating kiss known to man. When we've both exhausted any steam left in us, we fall apart, and he tucks me into his side.

The time glowing from the clock on the nightstand catches my attention. "Hey, Liam?"

"Yeah, baby?" he says, his voice groggy with sleep.

"Merry Christmas."

"Merry Christmas," he hums, then says, "And the answer is no, you're not opening a present early."

I scoff. "That's *not* even why I said it. And why would I

assume you got me anything? We didn't become an official couple until like five hours ago."

His lips rest at the back of my ear, and he takes a sleepy breath. "Because I saw you peeking at the wrapped boxes in my closet, and you are horribly impatient."

"*So* not true." So true.

"Holls, every year, you would sneak into your parents' room, open up all the gifts, and tape them back together."

"That was *one* year."

He sighs and snuggles me closer. "Whatever you say, Holls. Go to sleep."

I grumble under my breath and yawn. Maybe when he falls asleep, I'll sneak into his closet—

"Goodnight, Holls."

Ugh. Fine. "Goodnight."

"Oh, and, Holly?"

"Yeah?"

"I love you."

And just like that, he gives me the best gift ever.

epilogue

Christmas Day

Two years later…

"Pssst…baby, wake up."

"Five more minutes," I grumble, shoving my face farther into the pillow.

"I thought you were so eager to open your gifts?"

"I did last night. Now, I just wanna sleep."

His deep chuckle tickles the edge of my earlobe. "Taking off my clothes isn't unwrapping a gift."

"Okay, fine, can one of my gifts be to sleep five more minutes?"

"Get up, Bergner."

I roll over, taking in his sexy morning hair, happy eyes, and full lips. "That's *Mrs. Cody* to you, sleep thief."

He steals a kiss, his low growl waking up my libido. "Love the sound of that."

I love everything about this man. Our life.

One year ago today, we made promises to one another under Willow Falls' Christmas tree, for better or worse, in sickness and health. We let nothing hold us back in following our dreams. Liam followed through with his dream and started his journey to become a firefighter. And let me tell you, he is the sexiest firefighter. Liam helped me realize my worth, and with a little guidance from a financial advisor, I opened my own advertising business in town.

It's been a thrill of a ride already, and we haven't even scratched the surface of our forever.

Speaking of plans, a silly grin surfaces, and I raise my lips to brush against his. "Fine, you win. But I get to give out the first present. Don't move." I squirm out of his hold and disappear down the stairs. My heart skips a beat as I run to our enormous Christmas tree, bright, with a beautiful array of colors and ornaments. When we searched for our first home together, I had only one requirement: tall enough ceilings to accommodate an enormous tree.

I push through the cluster of gifts that weren't there when I fell asleep until I find the small box hidden in the back. When I make it back to our room, I jump on the bed and straddle Liam.

"What's this?"

"It's a pony! Open it."

"We said no gifts."

I laugh at that one. "Says the tree downstairs magically piled to the brim with them."

Liam chuckles softly. "Are you saying the magazine cut out of the KitchenAid mixer wasn't a hint?"

I shrug. That mixer better be under the tree. "Just open it. If it makes you feel any better, I didn't spend any money on this one."

He eyes me suspiciously. "It's not *that*," I say about the gag gift I gave him for his birthday. "And you liked it, so shut up."

"I would have liked it more if you hadn't lost the key."

Whatever.

I push him to hurry up. My pulse quickens as he pulls at the ribbon. He opens the box, and I stare intently at his face, watching, waiting...

His stomach muscles tighten as he takes in my gift, his eyes glued to the box. He takes too long to respond, and I worry this is going south. His mouth parts. His Adam's apple bobs. "Not as good as the handcuffs?" I ask, my voice shaky.

His gaze lifts to mine. He clears his throat, blinking away tears. "Are you...?"

"About to get really fat and moody? Yes."

Liam drops the box holding my positive pregnancy test and grabs my cheeks, pulling my lips to his. "I'm gonna be a dad. . ." Drawing in a deep breath, he kisses me harder. Then he scares the hell out of me when he hollers to the ceiling, "I'm going to be a fucking dad!" Happy tears shed down both our faces as he flips me under him. The way he looks down at me with so much love creates a warmth in the deepest part of me. "Thank you."

I giggle against his lips. "What are you thanking me for? It's kind of a shitty gift. I mean, you did partake in half of it, so it's half yours, half mine."

"For being the reason my heart beats. Bringing happiness into my life. Loving me." He spreads little pecks over my face. "Thank you for giving me the best Christmas present a man could ever receive."

Okay, he got me there. My eyes dance with unshed tears as I look up at my soulmate, my husband, the soon-to-be father of my children. With a full heart, I reply, "I better have gotten that mixer. . ."

epilogue

T *hree years later…*

"Seriously, you need to start thinking of other gifts to give him," Kelly Anne laughs over the phone.

"I know. I mean, how lame to always get Henley shirts and pregnancy tests." I sigh. What I need to do is find some self-control.

"Hey, if I had a husband who looked like that, I'd be poppin' out babies left and right too."

Nine months after I gave Liam my present, Nicholas was born. He was all Liam in the looks department with my attitude and the present that kept on giving. His laughter, his quirky little faces, his determination… he was perfect.

When I handed Liam another box the next Christmas, he was just as ecstatic. We both cried. Our family was growing.

"I mean, you didn't give him one last year. Does that count?"

"True. And it disappointed him when he opened the small box with the set of keys to a new truck instead of another test."

"See! Your man is perfect, and he wants you all plump and making his babies. I'm happy for you, but please tell me you're going to practice some self-control after this one. You're way more fun when you can drink."

I tsk at that statement. "I'm pretty sure the last two times were because I'd been out drinking with you!" Downstairs, Nicholas chants, "Presents!" while Noel cries. "I gotta go. I hear Noel's hungry cry."

"Good luck. Give my little niece and nephew a big kiss from their auntie. Feel free to slap one on your man for me too."

I laugh. "Will do. Merry Christmas." I hang up and take a few deep breaths. I brush my fingers along my belly, an overwhelming sense of joy in my heart.

"Joy," I whisper the name. "I think that will be perfect." My eyes fill with happy tears. "Miracle doesn't sound too bad either, does it?"

I grab the small worn box from my closet and head downstairs, prepared to give my husband the best Christmas gift or a heart attack.

Because inside the box, there are two tests.

We're having twins.

THE END

If you enjoyed Holiday Ever After check out my strangers to lovers romantic comedy Lake Redstone!

join the club

Want to hear about new releases, sales, exclusive content, and wine memes? Join my bi-monthly newsletter.

Want access to the more day to day happenings which also includes exclusive content, games, and giveaways? Join my reader group CLUB JD

Want to be notified when I have a sale or freebie? Check out Bookbub.

acknowledgments

To myself. It's not easy having to drink all the wine in the world and sit in front of a computer writing your heart out, drinking your liver off and crying like a buffoon because part of the job is being one with your characters. You truly are amazing and probably the prettiest person in all the land. Keep doing what you're doing.

Second most important, thanks for *nothing* to my toddler who made this book take forever to finish because he's so damn needy. Momma loves you.

I can't scream loud enough, a HUGE Thanks to all my eyes and ears. Having a dedicated squad who has your back is the utmost important when creating a masterpiece. From betas, to proofers, to PA's to my dog, Jackson, who just gets me when I don't get myself, thank you. This success is not a solo mission. It comes with an entourage of awesome people who got my back. So, first and most important, shout out to my homegirl Gina Behrends—you are literally the reason I know what day it is, and for that I love you. Thank you for being the best wingman anyone could ever ask for. You're the true celebrity here.

To my insanely amazing betas and proofers—Jennifer Lee Kreinbring, Jenny Hanson, Molly Witman, and Sierra Miller. You all have such an amazing eye, and my books are what they are because of you. To Kristi Webster for being my boo. To my street team/Review team and anyone who I may have forgotten! I appreciate you all!

Thank you to Monica Black at Word Nerd Editing for helping bring this story to where it needed to be.

A screaming thanks to Molly at Novel Mechanic for having superb insight and proofing. Everyone should have you on their side!

Thank you to All By Design for creating my amazing cover. A cover is the first representation of a story and she nailed it.

Thank you to my awesome reader group, Club JD. All your constant support for what I do warms my heart. I appreciate all the time you take in helping my stories come to life within this community.

And most importantly every single reader and blogger! THANK YOU for all that you do. For supporting me, reading my stories, spreading the word. It's because of you that I get to continue in this business. And for that I am forever grateful.

Cheers. This big glass of wine is for you.

about the author

Best-selling author, J.D. Hollyfield is a creative designer by day and superhero by night. When she's not cooking, event planning, or spending time with her family, she's relaxing with her nose stuck in a book. With her love for romance, and her head full of book boyfriends, she was inspired to test her creative abilities and bring her own stories to life. Living in the Midwest, she's currently at work on blowing the minds of readers, with the additions of her new books and series, along with her charm, humor and HEA's.

J.D. Hollyfield dabbles in all genres, from romantic comedy, contemporary romance, historical romance, paranormal romance, fantasy and erotica! Want to know more! Follow her on all platforms!

Made in the USA
Middletown, DE
01 October 2023

39624444R00086